The Guns of Redemption

THE GUNS
OF
REDEMPTION

James Wesley

AVALON BOOKS
THOMAS BOUREGY AND COMPANY, INC.
22 EAST 60TH STREET • NEW YORK 10022

PRINTED IN THE UNITED STATES OF AMERICA
BY THE BOOK PRESS, BRATTLEBORO, VERMONT

CHAPTER ONE

Joel Badly stopped his horse in the grove of aspen on the hillside and looked down at the ranch house snuggled among the cottonwoods and pines in the bottom of the swale. The trees were tinged with autumn and the alfalfa fields up the draw had been sheared of their last crop. He squelched the surge of joy at the sight of the place, rebuking himself with the fact that he had only been gone a short time. To be exact, he had been in the penitentiary half a year, six months out of his young life. It was the reason for his being in the pen that galled him. Why his sentence had been cut from three years to six months he didn't know. Somebody had intervened on his behalf without giving Joel his name. Even the warden of the prison had refused to enlighten him, declaring that he had been sworn to secrecy.

1

"Take your freedom, son, and don't question the reason for it. Be thankful that your clothes, some money, and your six-gun was sent here for you. I'll give you your ten dollars separation dole the state so generously provides, but you won't be needing the cheap suit of clothes that goes along with it." The last was said with a touch of sarcasm.

"Keep the ten dollars too, warden. Buy some Bull Durham for the men inside," Joel had suggested.

The reason for his release might be a puzzle to him, but the events that had led to his incarceration were still sharp in his mind. His father, Bruce Badly, had always been a pushy man, straddling the line between virtue and sin just as he straddled the line between law and anarchy.

"The West ain't no place for mollycoddles, do-gooders, or turn-cheeks. When the Good Book was writ, it took no cognizance of rattlesnakes, gila monsters, nor scorpions. You cain't wait for them devils to bite you on one cheek 'cause you'll be a goner before they get to the other cheek. Keep trouble ten feet away, an' it won't do you no harm." That was the gospel his father had drilled into him since the birth of his memory.

Only his mother's advice had softened these harsh edicts. "Don't play God, Joel. There's two sides to every question and until both are heard, no judgment can be justified. A bullet shot in haste could make you repent until your dying day," she had cautioned.

"Kay," his father had objected, "you're puttin' the boy in jeopardy. Once a man sets his course, he's got to follow through or get a bullet in his own guts. This ain't Pennsilevany, or Virginny. This is New Mex, ten miles from the border of perdition, untempered by law an' order, with heaven plumb out of sight."

That was the code his father lived by, a code Joel was loath to accept. His older brother, Sam, didn't question their father's thinking. Sam followed his father in whatever course the older man set upon.

The fracas that had sent Joel to jail where his father was to languish for another four and one-half years, was a direct outcome of Bruce Badly's determination to settle things without regard for moral justice or the intervention of law. But the law had intervened in the form of U. S. Marshal Dean Peck whom Earl Giles had summoned all the way from Roswell on the Rio Hondo. The trial had been held in Roswell, at the time a growing cattle and wool center.

Joel could still remember the prosecutor's words as the trial opened: "The prosecution will prove that Bruce Badly shot and killed Jim Costly, Earl Giles's foreman, with undo provocation, and was aided and abetted by his son, Joel."

The provocation had been a water hole on Donega Creek, where Giles's half of the BB bordered on Badly's half of the BB. The names were misleading. Earl Giles and Bruce Badly were half-brothers, with different fathers but with the same mother. They had started out as partners in their youth with the backing of their mother, who had been generously endowed by her two husbands: Badly, who had been a cattle buyer, and Giles, who had been a lawyer. Their mother had learned something from both her husbands. From Badly she had learned sharp dealing but inside the law, and from Giles she had learned the tricks and loopholes that were the basic knowledge of every lawyer.

The half-brothers, on her advice, had bought up Spanish Grants, which had been honored by the United States at the treaty of Hidalgo. Following Richard King's example, they had hunted down the heirs to the grants, who were glad to sell for twenty-five to fifty cents an acre considering the land only fit for rattlesnakes and gila monsters. The two men prospered until after their mother had died. Then something had soured the partnership. Joel had been a youngster then and had never learned the real cause of the unfriendliness between the two half-brothers. But the partnership had continued in its own cool way.

Whatever the cause of the enmity, it had somehow helped land him in jail, along with his father. The trial jury had found Bruce Badly guilty of manslaughter instead of murder, because he had acted in the heat of passion. They had found him, Joel, an accessory to the killing. The judge had sentenced Bruce to five years in the penitentiary, and him, because of his youth, to three years.

For some reason the three years had been cut to six months. Why? He didn't know. His part in the fight had been purely one of reaction and loyalty. Perhaps the loyalty had been misplaced. For him the ordeal was over, and his heart swelled at the sight of the familiar ranch house that had been his only home. He clucked to the raw-boned cayuse he had bought with some of the money that had been sent him, and headed down the slant toward the stream with its life-giving water that nurtured this oasis of green in the vast expanse of brush, pinon, and stunted junipers.

"I reckon this is goin' to be your home, cayuse. We'll put some fat on your bones an' let you frisk with the remuda. I won't forget you even though I got me a prize gelding I called Volcan because he erupts like a volcano. I aim to surprise them at the house so we'll canter up through them chaparral swatches along the creek. Surprise 'em enough, an' I might learn who dragged me into the fight at the spring, or the name of the one who got my sentence cut down," he said to the plodding horse.

The horse nickered and plodded through the chaparral. In the rays of the setting sun, the sage on the hillside looked purple, and the sego lilies and Indian paintbrushes that defied the coming of autumn poked inquisitive faces up through the bunch grass. Before he was close enough to the house to hear the lowing of the cattle or the crowing of the cocks, he saw a shadow threshing its way through a screen of aspen. The shadow turned out to be a girl on a white pony, her hat hanging down her back, and her blonde hair trailing in the wind. He felt a strange surge of feeling at the sight of her, a feeling he had never experienced with her before. The girl with the golden tan and wide-set blue eyes was his cousin, Margo Giles.

"What do you mean, sneaking home like a fugitive?" she admonished him, her full red lips without humor. "I got your letter. I kept your secret."

Joel turned his head to hide the feelings that convulsed in him. He found his voice and held it steady. "What do you mean sneaking up on me like a she-cat ready for the kill?"

"Sneaking? Why you reprobate! I've been watching for you the last two days. I wanted to be the first to congratulate you. Not many reprieved convicts have a woman staunch and true waiting to greet them." She rode close to him, their knees touching, and held out her hands.

He hesitated. He remembered how soft and capable her hands were. Even though they were now confined in buckskin gauntlets, he shied away from contact with them. What he wanted to do was hold her in his arms and kiss her. He must be crazy, he told himself. She was his cousin, one to play and romp with as he had done over the years, but not one to fall in love with. He must never forget that.

"What's the matter, coz, have I suddenly become a leper?" she asked.

"Don't talk like that, Margo!" he reprimanded with a sharpness that surprised even him.

"Don't bite my head off. I have a reason for coming here and being the first to meet you. Can't we get down and sit on the ground like we used to?" she inquired.

He wanted to say no. It was apparent she didn't understand his feelings, his need to keep a distance from her. But he didn't want to alarm her. So, trying to act as casual and natural as possible, he swung from his horse to the ground without giving her a direct answer.

Without warning, she slid from her saddle into his arms, exclaiming "Catch!" as she did so.

Confused by the sudden contact with her, he let her slide through his arms, and she landed on the seat of her buckskin riding skirt.

"Why, you rat!" she exploded. "You used to help me down when I was little."

Joel's reply was without humor. "You're a big girl now, Margo."

"What difference does that make? I was a big girl before you went away to—to *prison*!" she retorted.

"You were strong enough to help me down then."

Joel held his tongue. What unaccountable difference did six months in confinement among hard and bitter men make? Why had his feelings toward her changed? He couldn't explain it himself. Something magic had been jarred loose in him at this first sight of her since his ordeal. He searched her honest face with its tip-tilted nose and wide blue eyes, and then he looked away, trying to put her out of his mind.

Her next action caught him off guard. She jumped up from the ground, brushed off her skirt, and threw her gauntleted hands about his neck. Then she kissed him. It was the same old cousinly kiss. But it upset him. And he broke her embrace roughly and backed away from her.

"What's the matter, Joel?" she queried in a hurt voice. "This is me, Margo, the girl you've taunted, teased, and wrestled all these years. What did they do to you in that horrid prison?"

"People change, Margo," he said unsteadily. "We can't go on being kids forever."

"But we can be friends forever, can't we, even if we are cousins?" There was a note of pleading in her voice.

"There comes a time, Margo, when cousins stop kissing," he told her.

She gave him an exasperated look. "What are cousins supposed to do, rub noses?"

"They're supposed to find somebody else to kiss," he replied.

"Oh, that! I've been kissed by somebody else," she said, surprising him.

It was Joel's turn to be exasperated. "By who?" he blurted out.

"By Pete Dana, the new foreman Pa hired after Jim Costly got killed in that fight at the water hole."

"Your pa hired a new foreman named Pete Dana?"

"That's what I said."

"I know Pete Dana, and you know Pete Dana, Margo."

"I knew of him, and I've seen him in Vado, swaggering around town with his toothy smile and invitation to trouble. Things have changed here since the showdown at the water hole. For a long time your father and his faithful son, Sam, have been pushing my father—your uncle—like two fighting bulls hogging grass. There have been bad feelings for years. But now it's worse than ever, and the partnership is finished. Your brother, Sam, is still calling your half of the land the BB. And my father is calling our place the Box-G, a brand he's registered with the marshal at Roswell. My pa don't trust Sam. He says Sam is out for revenge because of what happened to your father. Sam blames Jim Costly for having started the fight, and he has no love for the Box-G or my pa.

"Recently Sam finished fencing off the water hole that started the fight, and my father is demanding a fair split of the herd. To get a fair split he's hired a tough and pushy crew, confident that Sam is going to try and get the best of the deal."

"Let's get back to that kiss you gave Pete Dana," Joel said, mulling over what Margo had told him a few minutes earlier.

"I didn't give him a kiss. He caught me alone riding into the ranch, and he forced that kiss on me. It made me feel dirty inside. He threatened to do worse to me if I told my pa."

Her words ignited a fury in Joel he fought to control. The thought of Pete Dana forcing himself on her was a defamation not to be condoned. Her naivete was in itself an invitation to a man like Pete Dana, who was used to having his way with booze, bullets, and women. That Earl Giles would even hire Dana, or the men who stuck by him, was an indication of how swiftly and deadly the break between his father and his uncle had become. The confrontation had been festering for some time between the half-brothers, but it had never flared into violence until the showdown at the water hole. It was lamentable that Jim Costly had got killed in the showdown. He had been foreman for Giles before Joel had been born. When Earl and Bruce had married, they had set up their separate home ranches but continued to own the stock together, under the BB brand, sharing the profits.

Earl, perhaps egged on by Elsa, his attractive but aggressive wife, had begun to suspect that Bruce was cheating on him. It was peculiar that Giles, a quiet, thoughtful man, had married Elsa, who was outspoken, even truculent at times, and that Bruce, who was rugged, pushy, making his own law in the wilderness, had married Kay, who was kind, humorous, and Godfearing. It was said that opposites attract. These were two cases in point.

"If Dana ever lays a hand on you again, Margo, I'll kill him," Joel said grimly. "With my own two hands I swear I'll kill him!"

"And join your pa back in the pen, or on the end of a rope? I can take care of myself, Joel." She swept back the bottom of her buckskin jacket and exposed a knife in its sheath, hanging from her belt.

The sight made him even grimmer. "You wouldn't use that, Margo. You couldn't kill a man," he charged.

"No, but I could mark him plenty and brand him the son of Satan."

Joel shook his head. "Let's hope it won't come to that. I'm home now, I'll protect you."

She turned her face up to him, a look of despair in her honest blue eyes. He wanted to hold her, to banish the despair and stand between her and whatever adversity threatened her. When they were children and she scratched her knees or pricked her finger, it was he she went to, instead of her mother, for consolation and to be kissed better.

When they had raced their horses over the range, he had sometimes let her win on purpose, but she was never fooled. She had berated him for mollycoddling her, he remembered. They had got their learning in Vado, often riding double on the same pony from the schoolhouse. There had been few problems between them then other than petty spats. They went to dances together, she preferring his company to that of any of the other boys, but their relationship had never turned into romance. And it never could.

Margo broke into his thoughts. "I had reason for watching for you, for coming out here to talk to you before you see the others. Like I've been trying to tell you, there's a war starting between the Box-G and the BB, Joel. Sam is bitter about your father being sentenced for the killing of Jim Costly. My father is desolate over the death of Jim Costly, who had been with him for years before you or I were born. He's determined to get his share of the cattle and everything that belonged to the partnership, and to do so he has hired a gun crew at my mother's insistence. And to cap it all, he has forbidden me to see you ever again. That's why I sneaked out here to let you know what you had to face at home."

"You're never to see me again?" Joel inquired soberly. His emotions became numb.

"That's right. My mother wanted to send me away to a convent in Denver, but I won't go there. Denver is a long way off. We quarreled. I settled for a convent at Sante Fe, run by the nuns at the mission."

Joel was silent for a moment, trying to assimilate all this. Things had changed from what he had hoped to be a happy homecoming into the prospect of a range war between kinfolk who had once loved each other. It has been said that love and hate are separated only by a thin line, a very thin line. He couldn't quite comprehend it, although trouble and squabbles had been simmering over the past few years. The one thing he could comprehend was that he was losing Margo. There would be no more rides together, no more dances, no more tussling over the prize of an apple or whatever.

"I'll miss you, Margo," he said with feeling. "At least in the convent you'll be safe from men like Pete Dana." And, he thought to himself, safe from a cousin who has discovered his deep love for you.

"Don't look so glum, cousin. I'll be back for visits."

"But not to see me. Your mother will take care of that. Cousins can get too close, you know."

She looked at him wide-eyed, and he was aware of a subtle change in her. Her eyes became deep, lucid pools. A flush reddened her cheeks and her moist lips were parted showing the white line of her even teeth.

She gave him a gentle kiss. It was still a proper, cousinly kiss—but somehow with a difference.

"Perhaps it's a good thing that you're being sent away, Margo," he said, his throat dry.

"I never expected to care for you so much, Joel. Perhaps Mother suspected that I might get to feel this way."

Then, with tears in her eyes, she mounted her pony and rode off.

CHAPTER TWO

Joel rode up the arroyo keeping the trees between himself and the house as much as he could. As he neared the yard, the faint scent of the lingering roses and hollyhocks was still in the air. Down near the bunkhouse he saw Pop Keller, the bullcook, chopping wood. Pop was a fixture on the ranch. He had always seemed old to Joel, old and wise.

Joel rode past the house, heading for the pasture where a number of horses were being held for the coming roundup. He wasn't ready to meet his mother and whoever was in the house with her. He was still thinking of Margo.

Finally, he unsaddled his cayuse, rubbed him down with a handful of straw, and turned him into the

13

pasture through which the creek flowed. Then he doused his head in the water trough and raked back his reddish-blond hair.

In the corral beyond the bunkhouse he saw some strange men breaking in some broncs. Their talk that drifted to him was noisy and profane, and their handling of the wild horses was cruel and abusive. They must be some of the roundup crew Sam had hired. Bruce might have approved of Sam's choice, but to Joel it was a portent of trouble to come.

He made his way to the back porch of the solid adobe house with its thick walls that kept out the heat and the cold. It was a two-story structure with hand-hewn rafters and roofed with tiles baked by the Mescalero Apaches to a ruddy brown. The porch ran the length of the house. And above it was a balcony where one might sit and see the sunrise. He braced himself as he threw open the door and walked into the steaming kitchen that smelled of fresh-baked bread. The teakettle was hissing quietly on the stove.

His mother turned and looked at him, surprise and pleasure in her blue eyes. Her smooth face broke into a smile and she brushed back her long hair, the color of his own.

"Why—why, what in the world! How—how did you get here, son?"

Joel was surprised at the genuine bewilderment in her voice. She could not have been responsible for his shortened sentence, or if she were, she was concealing her feelings very well. The next instant, he was in her arms, kissing her fervently.

"They cut my sentence short, Ma. They wouldn't tell me why," he said when she had released him.

"Thank God you're free, son. You shouldn't have been sent up in the first place."

"Pa's still up there," he said soberly.

"Your pa was more culpable. He did shoot poor Jim Costly, whether he meant to or not. It was his hot temper that started the fight, they tell me. A stretch in the pen might sober him down some. He'll probably get out in two years, and we might have more peace and quiet on the range."

"I ain't so sure about that, Ma. I saw some proddy gents down in the corral breakin' in some broncs. The way they was cussin' an' mistreatin' them cayuses didn't sound like peace and quiet to me. And I hear that Giles has hired Pete Dana an' his crew as a rep on the roundup."

"Where did you hear that?"

He was not ready to disclose his clandestine meeting with Margo just yet. The next instant the decision was taken out of his hands. Sam Badly came into the rustic kitchen, slumped into a chair by the table, and blew the last of his cigarette smoke at the hand-hewn beams of the ceiling.

"Hi, Joel. I figgered I'd find you here," Sam said.

"How did you know I was home, Sam?" he asked, wondering if Sam might have had a hand in his release.

"I spotted our cousin Margo ridin' down the arroyo. She ain't been around here much since you went to jail. I kept an eye on her from the trees on the side of the hill."

Joel felt a jolt of apprehension. "You—you mean you spied on her?" he asked sharply.

"Of course. She's a danged purty filly. I don't blame you for huggin' an' kissin' her," Sam said slyly. "Fact is,

I've had a hanker to do the same, but I know better."

"What are you talking about?" Kay demanded, wiping her hands on her apron.

Joel took over the conversation before Sam could make any more snide remarks. "Margo met me as I was comin' up along the creek hoping to surprise you. She wanted to tell me how things had changed here in the six months I've been gone. She told me about her pa hirin' a tough crew for the roundup, ramrodded by Pete Dana. She said it was shaping up into a range war."

"What else did she tell you?" Kay asked.

"She didn't have much chance to tell him anythin' else, Ma. They was too busy huggin' an' kissin'," Sam said in a taunting voice.

Kay turned her eyes away from Sam. "Is that true, Joel?"

"Not like it sounds, Ma," he said. "She told me that Pete Dana had forced himself on her and had threatened to do worse than just kiss her if she told Uncle Giles about that forced kiss. I felt sorry for her. I promised to take care of her and see that Dana never again laid hands on her."

"Joel, boy, you don't mean you's gonna buck Pete Dana?" Sam jibed.

"I reckon I can draw as fast as Pete, or you, Sam. Even Margo can outdraw most men. God knows we practiced enough, her an' me, just to outdraw each other."

"I don't go around braggin' on my draw," Sam warned him, "an' I advise you to watch your mouth lest you aim to prod somebody to try you out. Anybody can learn a fast draw, but shootin' straight at a live target ain't for mollycoddles. How many men have you killed, Joel? Billy the Kid killed twenty-one men by the time he was twenty-one years old. You'll be twenty-one next month, that makes you twenty-one killin's short."

"Stop that kind of talk, Sam," Kay reprimanded him. "I haven't worked all these years to raise any Billy the Kids."

"I'm tellin' him for his own good, Ma. He could've kilt Jim Costly in that ruckus, but he left it up to Pa," Sam retorted grimly.

Joel saw a peculiar look cross his mother's face; it was a mixture of pain and remorse. Her eyes became watery-bright and he knew she was on the verge of tears. Her grief came from a gentle heart, though she had no blame in Costly's death. During Costly's infrequent visits to the BB, she had always been friendly with him, yet there had been an uneasiness in their friendship.

The cause of her uneasiness was never apparent to Joel except for the fact that his father was gruff and unresponsive when Costly and his mother were together. His father had been jealous, he realized that as he grew older, but he could see no cause for that jealousy. The memory of Margo's kiss abruptly came back to jar him. He suddenly realized how he would feel if another man made free with Margo.

"Pa killed Costly by accident," Joel said defensively.

"That ain't what the jury said. It was you who pushed Costly in the way of Pa's bullet!" Sam charged.

With painful clarity, the fight at the water hole flashed before Joel's eyes. The drought had made every water hole on the range important to the survival of the herd. The Donega Creek water hole was close to the unofficial border between the two halves of the ranch. Though the two half-brothers had been partners before the water-hole incident, there had been a lot of rivalry between them. Each of them tended a portion of the herd as if they weren't partners at all.

Anyway, Bruce Badly had decided to build a drift fence that would guide his portion of the cattle to the water, and keep out Giles's portion. In a way this didn't make sense because every year they shared the profits from the total herd, straight down the middle. But since when did orneriness have to make sense?

When Giles had got word of the project, he'd sent Jim Costly out to see what was going on. By the time Jim arrived, the fencing wire and posts were already on the site. Some Mexican laborers were digging postholes and others were rolling out the barbed wire. Joel and his father were mounted side by side as Costly rode up alone.

Costly demanded to know what Bruce was doing.

"I need this water for the cattle on this end of the Tularosa Range," Bruce had told him. "I aim to build a fence to protect it."

"Wait a minute, Badly. You ain't talkin' quite clear. This water hole is on open range. Besides, you and Giles are supposed to be partners. What right have you to hog it?"

"I make my own rights here, Costly. Giles can count on the Wolf Spring Slough for water, up at the other end of the range," Bruce had barked.

"The Wolf Spring has dried up an' the slough is mostly scum, you know that, Badly," Costly had countered.

There followed a heated argument in which names

were called and accusations made about things Joel
had never heard of.

"You're not playin' God, Bruce, you're playin' the
Devil. I've watched the way you've treated Kay over the
years, blamin' her for things that you brought on
yourself. Now you're takin' out your spite on Earl, your
half-brother. You got something in your craw you can't
spit out." Costly had charged.

Joel, alarmed at the heat of the argument, had
started toward Costly to calm him down before Bruce's
temper exploded. The Mexicans had stopped their
labors and stood watching the quarrel.

"Mebbe you put the bone in my craw, Costly.
Getting rid of you might get rid of the bone!" Bruce had
charged.

"You ain't drivin' me outta here, Bruce," Costly had
retorted, his lips tight and his eyes puckered. "Every
man suffers for his own sins. I can live with mine. Yours
is still gnawin' on you."

"Damn you, Costly! I ain't takin' no sass from you!
Next time you come to the house smirkin' over Kay, I'll
kill you!"

The charges and counter charges made no sense to
Joel, but he knew his father's temper. Bruce had killed
men before, men who had got in his way when he was
hogging the range. Costly had reached behind him, his
hand closing over the grip of the blacksnake whip that
hung from the cantle of his saddle.

Joel saw the tremor of Bruce's shoulder, the sign that
he meant to draw. Hoping to drive Costly out of the
way of a bullet and prevent a tragedy, he lunged his
horse at Costly. Bruce's gun roared and the tragedy he
had tried to prevent happened. Instead of forcing

Costly out of range of the bullet, he had pushed him into the path of it.

The ensuing tableau was still clear in his mind. Costly dead on the ground, the Mexicans crossing themselves and staring in wide-eyed terror, and his father looking stupidly at the smoking muzzle of his gun.

At the trial the Mexicans had been the only witnesses. They had little understanding of the quarrel. They testified with unshakeable candor that Bruce had drawn the gun on an unarmed man, and that Joel had pushed the victim into the path of the bullet. Bruce's testimony that he had intended only to shoot the whip out of Costly's hand, and Joel's testimony that he had tried to push Costly out of the way of a bullet, sounded vague and evasive against the testimony of the peons.

For Joel the worst of the tragedy was over, but his mother still carried the emotional scars of the trial and convictions. Although she had tried a moment ago to be philosophical about Bruce's imprisonment, he knew that the tragic affair had marked and aged her. Costly's untimely death had added to her sorrow. She had been friendly toward Costly, although sometimes she seemed reluctant to show her friendship because of Bruce's jealousy.

"What's done is done," Kay said with finality. "Now you've got to pick up where you left off, son. With your pa gone, it's up to you and your brother, Sam, to share the responsibilities of the BB. Someday you boys will own the ranch, so see that it's taken care of properly."

Sam stood up and stretched, running a hand through his tousled black hair. An amused smile ruffled the bony structure of his rugged face. "Did the warden say whether your sentence was commuted, or did he say you was pardoned?"

Joel gave Sam a hard look, trying to read his reason for the question. "He didn't say neither. He just said I was free to go. Anyway, what difference does it make, Sam?"

"It could make a lot of difference, Joel."

"I'm free either way, ain't I?"

"You're outta jail, but unless you got a full pardon, you're still a felon. A felon ain't got the same rights as other men. He's lost his right to vote. He cain't own property. I reckon that once a man's convicted of a felony, he becomes an outcast like a leper." There was a jeer in Sam's voice.

"Shut up, Sam!" Kay ordered. "You're treating your brother like a criminal in his own home. At least you could let him get a few moments' pleasure out of his freedom."

"He's already had his few moments of pleasure down by the creek, Ma," Sam said. "You coddle him if you want to, but we ain't in a coddlin' situation. Uncle Earl is plenty riled up over the death of Jim Costly. Now we're gonna split up the herd. And he don't trust us, and I reckon I don't trust him. Earl has hired men who are more handy with a gun than they are with a rope. I aim to match him man for man, includin' Pete Dana."

With that, Sam went out. Joel stood staring at the closed door. Sam sounded just like their father; meet force with force. There had to be some way to prevent an open fight between the two ranches that had once been so close.

Kay interrupted his thoughts. "What *did* happen down at the creek, Joel? I'd like to hear your side of it. I know you wouldn't cover up or lie to me."

"Ma, I ain't sure what happened. When I left here, me an' Margo was still friendly cousins. Bein' holed up for six months in that ungodly federal pen in Yuma, with killers an' bandits for company, opens a man's eyes to the joy of freedom an' the value of love an' friendship. There was nothin' there but cages with barred doors an' iron cots with straw. We ate whatever slop they offered us and stared out at the thousand miles of desert that was more confining than a stone wall. It took me four days to reach Las Cruces an' another day to get here.

"When I saw Margo lookin' so pure an' beautiful, something jarred loose inside of me. I never knew exactly just what love was until that moment, Ma. It made me feel warm an' wonderful, but empty inside with an emptiness only she could fill. That's the only way I can say it."

Kay nodded. "You've said it beautifully, son. I've watched you two grow up together, even though Margo was younger than you by four years. I was afraid this might happen, but I hoped common sense might intervene. I should have known that common sense and love have nothing in common. I, of all people, should have known that," she said in a pensive voice. "Did Margo discover your love for her?"

"Not at first. She had come out to meet me so that she could explain how things were here, so that I could prepare myself to face them. I got off my horse an' she slid into my arms like she did when we were kids. I didn't dare hold her. I let her slip through my arms and she fell on her bottom. She got madder'n a wet hen. We gabbed some more. She told me her pa forbade her to see me anymore an' that her ma was sending her away to school."

"Perhaps that's a good thing, son. Elsa might be more perceptive than me in the ways of love. Where is she sending her?"

"She meant to send Margo to Denver, but Margo balked at the idea. They settled on a convent in Santa Fe. Anyhow, we kissed—and though I might never see her again, I just can't stop thinking about her."

Kay said, in a choked voice, "First love is like that, Joel. It hits you hard. But you'll get over it, and there'll be other loves in your life. You'll find a true love, a girl who's meant for you, a girl who'll become your wife someday. Try to forget Margo, son, think of other things."

"I reckon there's the roundup to think about. And I aim to take my part in the roundup, felon or no felon. Perhaps I can stop another tragedy from happening."

"Just don't get yourself killed, son. Sam needs your steady hand."

"Is it true what he said about my bein' a felon with no rights like other folks?"

"That's the law, Joel. I hope it doesn't apply to you."

"Whoever got my sentence cut down ought to know about it. If they wanted to do me a favor, they should've got the *felon* off my name."

A strange look crossed Kay's face and her blue eyes clouded. "I just had another weird thought, Joel."

"What is it, Ma?"

"Some people didn't agree with the sentence the judge handed down. They figured you were just as culpable as Bruce. They figure the both of you should have been hanged. There was only one way they could change that sentence."

"How's that, Ma?"

"To get you out of prison so they could kill you!"

CHAPTER THREE

Earl Giles, his brown hair spread over the balding spot on his head, scratched one of his outstanding ears and faced the men he had called together in the Box-G bunkhouse. The long, dingy room smelled of wet chaps, stale manure, and cigarette smoke. Giles was a direct opposite of his half-brother, Bruce. He was a man given more to thought than to action. Impulsive action often led to trouble or defeat. A plan well thought out, with the moral and legal aspects given consideration, was more likely to bring success in the long run.

Bruce and he had gotten along well enough when there had been just the two of them. Bruce had been the muscle and he had been the brains. Not that he didn't do his share of fighting off rustlers, digging longhorns out of the Big Thicket in the early days before they had gone in for pure-bred bulls to breed up the herd after the example of John Chisum, the cattle king of the Pecos.

But life has a way of bringing up complications a man can't get a handle on. He was still depressed over the killing of Jim Costly. Costly had been his right arm, taking orders without quibbling but not backing down if the occasion called for a firm stand. It was too bad Costly's last stand had to be against Bruce. With Bruce gone, that left Sam in charge of the BB, and Sam was as pushy and obstinate as Bruce, but without his father's experience. Now Sam had a chip on his shoulder, a big chip, maybe as big as a ripe fir log.

"I called you here, men, to explain what I expect out of the coming roundup. Most of the cattle on the Tularosa belong to the Box-G and the BB. The rounding up of the cattle will be done by you men and the BB crew led by Sam Badly. The one or two smaller ranchers will have representatives along to protect their interests. I ain't concerned with them. Sam Badly is naturally put out by his father's imprisonment and he might try to take out his spite on me. We'll have separate chuck wagons and camps on the range to cut down friction, but one of you men will ride with Badly's men to see they don't siphon off any cattle to be hid in the thicket until after the tally is made."

Pete Dana, his black hair swooping down over his squinty left eye, spoke up with his toothy grin.

"Are you, suh, givin' us free judgment in the use of our hahdware?" Dana asked in his Texas drawl.

"There'll be no shootin' an' no killing, Dana. Keep

track of the number of cows they cut out if you can, and report it to me. Understand?"

Dutch Leiberg, a skinny man who Dana had brought along, spat out his cud of tobacco and said, "We ain't goin' on no Sunday school picnic, boss. I been around proddy men before an' a slap on the wrist don't even annoy 'em. We got to make some protesting on the scene of the rustlin' even if it's jest a bluff."

"Well, don't push your bluff too far, Dutch. Somebody might call you on it," Giles warned.

"I don't get it, suh," Dana protested. "If Sam Badly tries to hide cattle right under our noses, we either got to make a protest or join in the rustlin'. You're payin' us good wages, an' we mean to earn them, but not by sittin' by an' watch you bein' cheated. I'm ramroddin' the crew or I'm not ramroddin' it. I'll take your orders up to a point, but I gotta have some lattytood in the mannah in which they's carried out. You knowed when you hired me, suh, that I ain't exactly no innocent preacher. The fat wages you're payin' is proof of that. Is it possible *you're* the one runnin' a bluff?"

Giles bristled. "How do you mean?"

"I reckon your placid attytood ain't genuine. You're payin' us fightin' wages to take care of trouble any way we can, but you want to stay free of all the blame."

"You're as much as callin' me a coward, Dana. If your purpose is to test me out, let it rest right here. I'm willing to stretch a point to stay out of trouble, not because I'm a coward, but because killing seldom solves anything. Jim Costly got killed in a fight over a water hole, that's what they say, but what really killed him was anger, pride, an' circumstances set up by those things."

"I've heard tell you're some kind of a lawyuh, suh. I reckon a showdown ain't no place fur logic. We won't start the pushin', but if Sam Badly starts to push we'll push back."

"I'm not askin' you to be martyrs, Dana. I don't expect any of you to die for the pride an' glory of the Box-G. I just want things run straight an' square. I hired you, Dana, an' your sidekicks, Leiberg an' Dobel, to show Sam Badly we mean business. My three regular men will fill out the crew and Wan Cho, the bunkhouse cook, will handle the chuck."

When Giles and his regulars left, Dana said, "Dutch, get that bottle you got stashed in your bunk. We got something to talk over, an' a shot of red-eye might sharpen our wits."

The bottle was passed around and Bull Dobel spoke up. "I reckon my wits is as sharp as they'll ever be. What's on your mind, Dana?"

"If we play our cards propah, we can make us a bonus outta this. We can let Sam Badly skim off all the cattle he thinks he can get away with. After the roundup, we'll beat Sam Badly to the thicket an' roust out them cattle fur ourselves. I know a reservation purchasing agent who'll be glad to take them off our hands for a discount under the price he's allowed to pay."

When Giles reached the low, rambling ranch house with its adobe walls and flat roof insulated with layers of earth to keep it cool in the hot summers and warm in the cold windswept winters, he found Elsa and Margo in heated argument.

The big living room smelled of the hand-tanned

buffalo hides that covered the crude but sturdy furniture constructed by the artisan Indians who had been trained by the padres at the mission near the reservation. The frames of the chairs, which were made from manzanita and ironwood, were lashed together with rawhide thongs which had first been soaked in water and then tightened as they dried into fastenings stronger than any glue.

He tossed his hat on one of the chairs and crossed the Navajo rug which covered the puncheon floor.

"Just a minute, Elsa," he ordered, raising his slim hand, "whyfore are you rawhidin' the girl?"

"I'm not rawhiding her, Earl, and she's not a *girl* anymore. Take a closer look at her. She went out to meet Joel Badly—"

Giles cut her off. "You mean Joel Badly's home—free out of prison?" He directed his question at Margo. "How did you find that out?"

Margo looked at him, her chin up, and a glint of defiance in her blue eyes. "I got a letter from him the last time I was in Vado. He wanted his homecoming to be kept a secret. Somebody interceded to get his sentence cut down, and he thought a surprise arrival might shock the truth out of his benefactor."

Giles scowled. "Who in hell would try to override the sentence of the court?"

"It wasn't you, was it, Pa?"

"Me? I wasn't even a witness at the trial."

"You could have had a twinge of conscience for calling in the marshal and having Bruce and Joel arrested and brought to trial."

"They confessed to the killing. They brought Costly's body here. I reckon they thought to get by on a plea of self-defense, but the story of the peons gave the lie to that. Bruce may be your uncle but he's been gettin' too big for his saddle. We gotta have law an' order here sometime. We can't let the top dogs go free an' hang only the mongrels."

"Are you sure, Pa, that there was no spite in your actions? I never did learn what turned you against the Badlys."

"It happened before you were born, Margo," Elsa said, brushing back her black hair. "Let's not rake over dead coals. Bruce and Joel were lucky they weren't charged with murder. The judge couldn't give them less of a sentence than he did for manslaughter. It was the jury who brought in the verdict."

"A jury sprinkled with their enemies," Margo retorted.

"Let's put the trial aside, it's over. You weren't arguing with the girl about that, were you, Elsa?" Giles asked.

"No, Earl. She sneaked out of here to meet him. Something happened out there that changed her. She left here a girl, and she came back a woman," Elsa said tightly.

"What kind of talk is that?" Giles inquired.

"You're a man, you wouldn't understand. She won't always be your little girl, Earl. Take a good look at her."

Margo stood before him defiantly for inspection. Earl took a good look at her and felt a weird, hurt feeling inside that could only be described as jealousy. It bewildered him at first. Her blue eyes did have a shining glow in them, and her face looked as soft and beautiful as the petal of a rose.

Earl's reaction was one of resentment. "I told you, Margo, when you carried on about Joel being sent to prison, to put him out of your mind and not see him anymore. I don't want you to have anything to do with those Badlys."

"Don't worry, Earl, she won't be seeing him again," Elsa said. "I'm sending her away to school where she will learn how to be a lady."

"What school, for God's sake?" Earl asked.

"I chose Denver, but we quarreled about that. We settled on Santa Fe. There's a convent at the old mission."

A mirthless smile curved Margo's lips. "I may become a nun," she said.

Earl broke down, put his arms around her, and held her close. "Things won't be the same around here without you, honey. I didn't count on your leavin' here. You're woman enough for me the way you are, but I ain't no judge of fine ladies. Mebbe your mother's right. It'll do you good, I suppose, to meet other people, do other things. You might find a real love in Santa Fe, a young man who can set you up in a fine house an' spare you the loneliness an' labor of ranch life."

"I haven't asked to be spared the loneliness and drudgery of ranch life, Pa. Ranch life is all I've known. I love the silence and vastness of the range, and to me nothing could be more boring than to sit in a big house wearing fine clothes and kowtowing to uppity people who might sneer at my ranch background behind my back. Some potbellied banker or businessman might marry me because I'm young and pretty, or one of their spoiled sons might hope to add me to their string of conquests. The older wives would be jealous and suspicious of me."

"You're inventing things," Elsa said without conviction. "I know some of those wives quite well, and I know the banker and his daughters. They're not as beautiful as you, but they know it and are honest about it."

"You'd be the queen of the cavvy, honey," Earl put in.

"Queens are like gunfighters, Pa, they're targets for attacks. I don't want to be a queen, I just want to be an honest wife raising a family for a man I love." She tried not to think of Joel Badly. "Someday I'll meet the right man. And when I do, I won't ask him how much money or power he has. We'll work for those things together, and I'll feel part of the success."

"It won't work around here, Margo," Elsa said solemnly. "You just won't meet the right man if you stay here on the ranch. Take my word for it. I know what I'm talking about. I was a young girl myself once."

"But you married Pa, didn't you?" Margo reminded her.

Elsa looked away. She said softly, "Your—your pa wasn't—wasn't my first love, either."

There was a moment of tense silence. Earl stood rubbing his chin, his eyes staring out the window. "I wasn't lookin' for no angel when I married your ma, honey. Angels don't belong on earth, their wings bruise too easy."

At that moment Dusty Kiler, one of Giles's regulars, came to the front door, which was covered only with the screen to keep out the buzzing horde of flies.

"Can I see you a minute, boss?" Dusty inquired.

"Sure, Kiler. I reckon I ain't gettin nowheres with this female chitchat. What's on your mind?" Giles asked, banging the flies off the screen before he went outside. They shared the bench on the long, covered porch that faced Elsa's enclosed garden with its pond of goldfish. The scent of jasmine spiced the air.

Kiler twiddled his hat in his lean hands and stared beyond the garden at the barren, gray cliffs of the Mesa Resonar which was so named because of the echoes that resounded from its stark sides.

"I'm a mite uneasy aboot Pete Dana an' his heel-dogs. Them three do a lot of jabberin' out of earshot. I ain't upset 'cause you gave him Costly's ramrod job. But if he gits too pushy, things might git unpleasant on the roundup," Dusty said.

"You was in the bunkhouse when I laid down the rules to Dana. No killin' an' no fightin' if we can help it. I figgered we needed a man with a tough rep to face up to Sam Badly. Sam's got a chip on his shoulder bigger'n a haywagon because of what happened to his pa. Sam might try to rawhide our crew, but I figger he'll stop an' think before he takes on Pete Dana an' his sidekicks. Did you know Joel Badly is home?"

"No. I ain't heard about it till now. What did he do, break jail?"

"No, Dusty, he was paroled out early. Somebody put in a word for him."

"Have you seen him? Is he riled up over that jail sentence, boss?"

"I haven't seen him, but Margo has. He didn't appear to be rambunctious to her," Earl said.

"Earl, one time you had a meetin' with Dana an' his

cronies whilst Oral Fibbs, Hebe Rasco, an' me was down in the harness shed gittin' our gear in shape. We don't know what went on then. But I figger if Dana is to be ramrod, that makes me *segundo*, the second man in the crew. You ain't makin' no deals with Dana without my knowledge, are you? I gotta know where I stand."

"No secrets, Dusty. Just what I told you, no killin' an' no fightin' unless Sam forces it."

"Did you tell Dana about the no-booze rule?"

"I reckon that's understood, it's the law of the range. No roundup was ever worth a damn with the men swillin' rotgut."

"They got a bottle stashed in the bunkhouse, boss. That's breakin' a bunkhouse rule, ain't it?" Dusty insisted. "They keep it to theirselves."

"That bottle stays in the bunkhouse. I'm not going to quibble over that rule right now," Giles temporized.

"Rules is like dominoes, Earl. If one rule goes down, they all go down. Dana makes his own rules like he done with Margo the other day."

"Wait a minute, Dusty. Explain that."

"He forced hisself on Margo. Got a big kiss before she could wiggle free."

"Margo never told me about that!" Giles snapped.

"Dana threatened to do worse to her if she blabbed."

Giles controlled his rising anger. The roundup was all set, there was little use to disrupt it because of a kiss. "I'll take care of Dana when the roundup's over. He won't get no chance to smirch Margo again. She's leavin' for a convent in Santa Fe. By the time the cattle's caught an' the brandin' done, she'll be gone."

"Okay, but you ain't clarified my position, boss. Am I to heel to Dana's commands, no matter what?"

"Dusty, I ain't askin' no man to demean hisself of pride or security. I'm just askin' you to not press a fight. If a fight is forced on you, I expect you to defend yourself with fists or bullets, whichever come first."

"I reckon I can abide with that, boss. I ain't ordinarily a brawlin' man. I ain't a gunslick neither— fact is, I've only kilt one man, a killin' I was absolved of by common consent. Ain't it a fact you're buildin' up an opposition against trouble that might not come?"

"The way I see it, Dusty, it's better to build a wall against trouble to keep it away. Once it starts, there ain't no time to take precautions."

"We allus got along with Bruce Badly, Earl, even though you an' him ain't exactly cozy no more. Sure, Bruce was pushy an' sometimes claimed more mavericks than he was entitled to, but pushy men are mostly men unsure of theirselves. They's scared to meet others on common ground for fear if they once lose the advantage, they'll be beaten."

"Simmer down, Dusty. I'm havin' a meetin' with Sam Badly to talk over the conduct of the roundup. I hope to come to an understandin' with him, but right now he's a proddy young man eager to make a good showin' to give his pa comfort."

Giles went back into the house to explain to Elsa and Margo that he was going over to the BB to talk to Sam Badly. He found Margo, her eyes red from weeping.

"What's the matter, honey?" he asked consolingly.

"You should know. You're kicking me out just like you did my older brother Orson three years ago," she retorted.

"We don't mention Orson around here, you know that," Earl said sharply.

"I know. I was just thirteen then and I forgot him, like you said, but he does exist. Just because he married an Indian girl didn't consign him to hell. Tonalea wasn't just an Indian squaw, Pa, she was an educated woman with pride and wisdom. I heard that the nuns at the mission school were proud of her."

"As I said before, there ain't goin' to be no squaw-man clingin' to the Giles's roots. I just nipped off the rotten wood."

"And now you're nipping me off, Pa. I'm sure I'll never make it back from Santa Fe."

"That was your ma's idea. She's determined to have one fine lady in the family."

"Isn't Ma a fine lady, Pa? I always thought she was," Margo mused.

"She's fine enough for me, Margo. Fact is, people get things stuck in their craw they can't hawk out. Some foolishment in their youth that haunts them. I ain't got time here to ponder on the past. I'm goin' over to the BB to discuss the roundup with Sam."

"Give Joel my regards," Margo said.

Giles met Sam in the yard of the BB ranch house, halfway between the barns and the bunkhouse. Men were busy down near the corrals, greasing the chuck-wagon wheels and soaking the water barrels in the water trough to make sure the staves were tight.

"Howdy, Sam," Giles greeted. "I come over to talk about the roundup. Where's Joel?"

Sam stood, his long legs planted a little apart. "Howdy, Earl. What fer you want Joel?"

"Margo sent him her regards," Giles said flatly.

"Ain't that a mite presumptious of her? She drove

him close enough to perdition with that kissin' an' huggin'. Joel's gone into town to find out if he has any friends left."

"Margo's leaving for a convent in Santa Fe, Sam. Joel won't have no need to fret over her anymore. I figgered Joel would be here an' we could talk over things together. He's got a half say-so on the ranch, ain't he?"

"Not exactly, Earl. Joel's still a felon in the eyes of the law. He ain't got no rights to hold property or cast his vote."

"Sam, you don't mean that, do you? You ain't goin' to let a legal technicality deprive Joel of his rights to the BB, are you?"

"Why not? You kicked Orson out because he married a squaw. Now you gotta hire gunslingers to ramrod your spread. Me an' Orson got along good together, but that crew you got now is prickly as a bee-stung bull. If you aim them to cow me down, I'm warnin' you I don't cowdown easy. I gotta prove to Bruce that the BB is in good hands. I won't settle for a short count."

"Neither will I, Sam. You got your crew backed up by some proddy gents yourself. I want no fightin' an' killin', Sam, just a fair count. This is the first time we aim to split the herd. Up till now we've only used the BB brand. This time we cut out the cows belongin' to the small ranchers, but the BB cows will be split fifty-fifty. I'll rebrand my share with a Box-G."

"That's goin' to be quite a job, Earl. Come into the house an' have a cup of java. Ma will be glad to see you."

CHAPTER FOUR

Joel Badly rode slowly toward Vado in the shank of the afternoon. Vado was a collection of flat-roofed adobes straggling between the stage road and the river. Vado meant *ford*. It was a good place to cross the river before it reached El Paso, in Texas. From El Paso south, the Rio Grande separated the United States and Mexico and it was a haven for cattle thieves, killers, and malcontents who still insisted that Texas was part of Mexico. Vado had a business center of sorts, and a bunch of two-story buildings topped with corrugated iron roofs.

One of the buildings was occupied by the Vado Queen, the busiest saloon in Vado, boasting the best beer and the best imported whiskey. And the dancing girls were the fanciest girls in town. It made no difference that the beer was cellar-warm or the whiskey laced with mescal. The heat of the day still hovered about the buildings and the stray dogs were still resting in the shade.

Joel pushed back his sombrero and sleeved the sweat off his forehead. There was a wariness in his blue eyes. His new cotton shirt was tucked into his Levi's. And his boots, in spite of the alkali dust, were shiny with their fancy stitching. His lean hips carried no gun. He remembered the warning his mother had given him: "To get you out of prison so they could kill you!"

A flaunted gun was an invitation to kill and an excuse for the result. If somebody wanted to kill him, unarmed, they would have to bear the stigma of murder. He reached the water trough in front of the general store and let his horse, Volcan, slake his thirst. An urchin, one of the few living things braving the heat, came up to him.

"I take care of your cayuse for you, meester. I weel take heem to the *caballeriza*, also rub heem down," the youngster said, hitching up his oversize trousers, which were frayed at the bottom and held up with a piece of rope.

"What's your name, *muchacho*?"

"Me Porferio Diaz, *senor*."

"Porferio," said Joel, slapping Volcan on the rump, "this is no cayuse. This is a *buena cavallo*."

"*Si, si, senor, mucho bueno*. Where is your *pistola*?"

"I left it home, *muchacho*."

"But, *senor*, much very *malo* hombres come here to Vado. What you do eef they shoot you, eh?"

"I'll die, Porferio."

"You *loco, senor*. You keel first, then you no *muerto*."

"I'll take care of myself, *muchacho*. Here's a peso. Take my horse to the livery barn, rub him down, an' see he gets plenty of hay, but only one can of oats, savvy?"

"*Mucho gracias*, much thanks!" Porferio exclaimed, staring at the shiny dollar in his small hand. It was apparently the biggest coin he had ever owned. "I weel feex your *caballo* up very *buena*. I weel stay weeth heem till you come. Eef you stay all night, I weel sleep weeth him. But eef you die, then what I do?"

"If I die, you can keep him, Porferio," Joel laughed. He had no intention of dying.

As the boy led the horse away, Joel looked up and down the street. A Mexican was hunched down sleeping in front of the hotel. He had a serape around his shoulders and his wide-brimmed sombrero was pulled down over his face. A dog lay sleeping beside him, his head on the Mexican's lap. Two *vaqueros* were riding into town from the direction of Ojinaga. An empty carriage was standing in front of the store near the water trough where Joel stood. Two women came out of the store wearing sunbonnets and flowery summer dresses. One was Emma Layton, the schoolmarm who had taught him and Margo all through elementary school. The other was a young woman about Margo's age, with a wealth of auburn hair flowing from under her sunbonnet and a face that looked very fair among the swarthy or suntanned faces prevalent in New Mexico. Emma looked at him in startled surprise.

"Why—why, Joel! I thought you were in—in jail," she said hesitantly, glancing at the young woman beside her.

"Somebody took pity on me an' got me out," he said dryly.

"That was a horrible affair, the shooting, I mean. Some people still think you were guilty. I never did. I believed your story."

"You didn't get me released, did you, Emma?"

"I had no way to do that, Joel. I would have got you exonerated completely if I could. But let's not discuss the unpleasantness before Dorothy. This is my young niece, Joel. I'm going back to Boston to wallow in my memories. To Dorothy the thought of teaching out here in the wild West sounded exciting. She insisted on relieving me. So far her spirits are undaunted."

"I'm happy to meet you, Joel. My girlhood dream was to come West and meet a cowboy."

"Thank you, ma'am, but you ain't getting your wish with me. At the moment I'm an ex-jailbird set loose through somebody's sympathy, or their desire for revenge. To be seen with me is dangerous. You're too fair-skinned for the sun and too beautiful for the scenery. Take a look around an' go back to Boston, or wherever."

"Well, well, I must say you're outspoken," Dorothy said, with a smile exposing white, even teeth. "Outspoken and presumptuous. On our first meeting you flatter me in one breath and dismiss me with the next. I may sound vain, but most men prefer to keep me around."

"Most men in Boston or wherever. Out here, Miss Layton, you'll run into men who would prefer to express their feelings in ravishment," Joel said solemnly.

"My, what a choice of words. Ravishment. Did Emma teach you that?"

"Jest statin' a fact, ma'am."

"Well let me further your education. Men are men everywhere with the impulses of nature, and ravishment, as you call it, is just as prevalent in Boston, whether it comes in a formal dress suit with white tie, or a pair of dungarees. Most men, regardless of how chaste they were reared, ravish a young woman in their minds."

"Such talk!" Emma remonstrated. "We can't stand out here in the hot sun, speculating on the primitive impulses of the male animal. Dorothy will be staying with me until I leave. Perhaps you can continue your conversation at a later date. Right now, Joel, I'm sure you're dying for a beer."

"And don't worry about me," Dorothy said in parting. "I'm a sorceress myself."

Without a word, Joel helped her into the carriage and watched them drive away. He thought of Margo. He could never ravish her. And he turned, heading for the Vado Queen. Two cowboys came out as he neared the door. They wore warped, sweat-stained hats and had three days' growth of whiskers bristling on their lean jaws. One was smoking a poorly rolled quirly that was spilling tobacco down his chin. The other was mouthing a chaw of tobacco. They were typical cowboys just in off the range not yet shaved and deloused. Joel grinned inwardly. If Dorothy Layton were here now, she might change her mind about going back to Boston.

"Howdy, hombre," one of the men said as he passed them.

The men gave him a hard look and he wondered if they had been at the trial that had convicted him.

"Howdy, men. It must be hell out in the chaparral on

a day like this."

"Only a mite hotter, amigo," the first man said, continuing to stare at Joel.

"Anything wrong?" Joel asked, and braced himself for the answer.

The man scratched his lean jaw. "Nothin' wrong, I reckon. You're a dead ringer for a man I saw up in Roswell a few months back. You couldn't be him, though. He's sweatin' out three years in the federal pen in Yuma."

Joel made no response as the men ambled on around to the shady side of the building to mount their horses. So he was already recognized. On an impulse he crossed the dusty road and stepped into the store labeled, *Dressmaking and Ladies' Necessaries.* It was hot in the store, which smelled of incense that sweetened the odor of old yard goods still waiting to be sold. The woman fanning herself behind the counter dropped her fan and stared at him.

"Why—why Joel! How, why..."

"Don't get flustered, Hilda, it's me all right. My jail sentence was cut short."

"How did that happen?"

"I ain't sure. Even the warden couldn't answer that. As Ma said, either somebody loves me or hates me. I've come into town to find out which."

"Why would anybody intercede to get you out of jail if they hated you?"

"There's a logical answer to that question, Hilda. Some people didn't agree with the sentence Judge Cottle handed out. Accordin' to Ma, they might want to change it with a six-gun."

"You mean murder you?" Hilda said, aghast.

"It won't look like murder when it comes. I reckon I'll be squeezed an' taunted into a shootout by some gunny hired for the purpose. I'll be dead, the gunny will claim self-defense, an' the hombre who hired him will still be a mystery."

"My goodness! Why did you come back here, Joel? Why don't you go to another territory where they never heard of the trial?"

"I came back here 'cause this is my home, for one thing. For another, I ain't partial to dodgin' trouble. A man takes his troubles with him. They stick to him like a bur under his shirt. How have things been with you, Hilda?"

She gave him a blank look. "You've only been gone for six months, Joel. I haven't had time to go broke, get sick, or be married—if a man should ask me."

"Any man would be proud to have you, Hilda. You're still a good-looking woman. What happened to Cy Madson shouldn't spoil the rest of your life. Cy got shot for dealin' off the bottom of the deck."

"Yeah. I know, Joel. I got one of his shady deals. I'm Cy Madson's widow, the former wife of a gambler who played a crooked game. Cy left me with marked cards, and I'm not smart enough to lay down my hand."

"Don't belittle yourself, Hilda," Joel said, and then his mind was taken off the subject by what he saw through the shop window. He had come into the shop to spy on whoever entered the Vado Queen.

It was cooling off outside and people were moving about. Three men emerged from the shaded alley beside the saloon. Joel stiffened as he recognized them. Pete Dana, with his shaggy hair and bashed-in sombrero. He wore his single-action Colt .44 strapped to his bowed leg. Joel had seen him fan that gun once in a shootout. There were no distinct shots, only a blur of sound. His two heel-dogs were with him: Dutch Leiberg, with his emaciated stomach bisected by the cross-belts he wore to hold his twin holsters, and Bull Dobel, with his short legs bowed to the shape of a horse's belly.

Joel swallowed hard to ease the dryness in his throat. He thought of Dana forcibly kissing Margo, and a red film swam before his eyes. To walk into the Vado Queen, with his gun on his leg, could provoke an instant confrontation. It was unthinkable that Dana had got his sentence reduced. Not the territorial governor, Henry Demargo, or Judge Cottle would accede to any request Pete Dana made. But whoever made the request for his release could have hired Dana as the executioner. Joel ran his tongue across his thin lips. Hilda was watching him, reading his thoughts.

"You're not in trouble with Pete Dana, are you, Joel?" she asked softly.

"I ain't quite sure, Hilda, but it's a likely prospect."

"You're unarmed. There's three of them."

Joel nodded, pulled his hat down securely on his light red hair. "I'm unarmed on purpose, Hilda. I want to avoid gunplay. I don't know who's with me or against me. I've got to make some inquiries before the gun-talk starts. Wish me luck, Hilda."

"A fool needs more than luck to survive in hell, he needs a miracle. *Vaya con Dios*, is the best I can do, Joel."

"I reckon God won't have much to do with what's goin' to happen, Hilda."

With that he walked out into the street, which was

busy with freight wagons from the mines, buggies bringing women in for shopping, and a group around the stage office waiting for the afternoon stage to arrive. The smell of dust and horse dung was kicked up by the plodding hooves. He made his way to the opposite side of the street and paused to get a grip on himself. He had to face the music. Pete Dana was going to be on the roundup.

Why Giles had hired Dana and his henchmen was a mystery in a way. It was out of character for his uncle to foster trouble. Elsa Giles he understood. She had no aversion to force. She'd probably influenced Earl. And the breach between Earl and his father had certainly widened, and the tension had clearly built up since his incarceration. The death of Jim Costly had been a blow that might embitter a man like his uncle. It had been a blow that even Joel and his mother had felt deeply. Sam Badly had taken the court's decision as a personal affront, and Sam was a replica of their father. Somehow the edge had to be filed off the friction that threatened the two halves of a ranch that had once been a harmonious partnership. He might as well start filing on that edge now.

Joel walked resolutely up to the doors of the Vado Queen, shoved them open, and slid quickly inside. At first no one noticed him. He scanned the line of men at the bar and those at the card tables getting ready for the evening's play. There was no mistaking Dana at the bar, his warped hat tipped back on his shock of black hair. He was in the center of the line making his usual big talk punctuated by the horse laugh that showed his buck teeth. Dutch Leiberg and Bull Dobel were on either side of him.

"I reckon I got me a honest job this time. Straight ridin', an honest count, an' top money—that's what Giles wants," Dana said with a smirk. "We's gonna put salt on them dogies' tails an' ease 'em onto the brandin' circle. If we find renegades off'n the reservation, we politely show them the errah of theah ways an' send 'em home. Theah ain't goin' to be friction twixt us an Sam Badly. I ain't sure Sam heard about that, though."

There was a rumble of laughter among the men. Joel looked about the room taking in its bullet-scarred adobe walls and getting his lungs used to the smells of spilled liquor, stale tobacco smoke, and the faint odor of perfume wafting from the three dance girls in their scanty costumes, who were seated around one of the tables idling away the time with a game of euchre while they waited for the evening's action to begin. Meg Easter was at her post at the end of the bar, watching the trade straggle in. Meg was half owner of the bar, looked after the girls, and kept the roughhousing down to a minimum.

Meg was one of Joel's friends and mentors. She had taught him how to handle his liquor after his first disastrous drunk at the age of sixteen. She had cautioned him against bragging about women, horses, or guns. He still counted her as a friend and decided to talk to her first. He started toward her through the haze of tobacco smoke, keeping well behind the men at the bar who were too engrossed with their loud talk and booze to notice him. When he was halfway across the line of men, a drunk staggered away from the bar and bumped into him.

"Whatsa matter with you, hombre? Cain't ya see where yoush goin!" the drunk said, mouthing a curse that could be heard across the room.

Before Joel could answer or make a pacifying apology, Dana turned his head and stiffened.

"My Gawd!" Dana croaked. "Look who's heah!"

The men at the bar turned in unison.

Dutch Leiberg stared goggle-eyed. "Why—why thet's Joel Badly, the jasper who set Jim Costly up for killin'!"

Bull Dobel twisted his big head on its short neck. "How come you's footloose, Badly? They say nobody gets outta that Yuma prison an' lives to cross the desert. Did you break jail? Mebbe we'll git a reward fer turnin' you in."

Joel kept a tight rein on his emotions. He backed off and stared at them. "Somebody begged, bought, or borrowed me out of Yuma without sayin' why. If it was a friend, I want to thank them. If it was somebody settin' me up for a target, I want to know who it was."

Dana moved a foot away from the bar. "Got any idees on the subject, Mistah Badly?"

"I reckon it was somebody who didn't agree with the verdict of the court or the sentence handed down by the judge," Joel said calmly.

Dana brushed his swooping hair out of his eyes. "I didn't agree with the judge *or* the jury, Mistah Badly." His voice was brittle.

"An' I didn't neither," Dutch Leiberg seconded.

"Have you come heah for a trial with bullets?" Dana goaded him.

"That wouldn't solve anything, Dana. I just want to know why I was turned loose, whether through friend or enemy," Joel said quietly. He knew he was baiting the devil.

"I reckon a friend would come forward peaceable,

Badly. An enemy might not want to be known. He might hire an executioner—like me, for instance." Dana kept his voice level. "Mebbe we can rectify the mistake of the court, right heah an' now. Then you'll have your answer."

"I didn't come here for gunplay, Dana. I'm not armed."

"No problem, Badly." Dana jerked his head at Dutch Leiberg. "Dutch, toss him a gun!"

Joel crouched. The loaded gun arched toward him. The gun spun over his shoulder untouched. Joel threw himself aside as Dana's gun roared. The bullet whistled past his head and buried itself in the adobe wall. He braced himself for the impact of a second shot. The second shot never came. Meg Easter, a pearl-handled derringer in her slim hand, took charge.

"That was one of your lousiest tricks, Pete. You kill him and it's murder pure and simple. Take my word on it. If you want to carry the trial further, do it in a fair fight. That is, if you've got the guts, Pete."

Meg Easter's taunt from the end of the bar was like the lash of a whip to Dana. He unbuckled his gunbelt and let it fall to the floor. He crouched for the attack. "I reckon I'll get my satisfaction in blood and skin!" he snarled.

The men in the room moved away, clearing the center of the floor. Instant wagers were being made on the outcome before the first blow was struck. Joel leaped to his feet from the half-prone position he had had to assume to dodge Dana's bullet. He knew what he was in for. He had been cornered into a vicious fist fight with a bruiser while in Yuma Prison. He had managed to hold his own with the big man until the guards broke up the fight. He had been hurt in that fight, but the hurt had been worth the effort. Now he crouched, balanced on the balls of his feet, to meet Dana's charge.

CHAPTER FIVE

Dana, frustrated in his gunplay and stung by Meg's remarks, barged in like a wild bull loosed from the chute. His big fists were pumping like crazy and his shaggy hair drooped into his glaring eyes. Joel waited for the attack, timing his move. Dana's fist came at him, and Joel danced aside. Dana's momentum was unchecked as his fist pawed the air. He lost his balance and fell forward to his hands and knees. A guffaw of laughter went up from the circle of men.

"Watcha doin', Pete, prayin'?" one man yelled.

That was all it took to drive Dana berserk. He got up, snorting. He saw Joel standing to one side with a half smile on his lips. He barged at Joel, head down, spittle drooling from his mouth. Joel took a jarring blow to the shoulder, another that slid off the side of his bobbing head.

Dana had his head down to butt Joel in the guts. Joel raised his knee sharply and smashed it into Dana's down-turned face. Blood spurted from Dana's nose and the spittle on his mouth turned red. Joel knew he was goading the devil. The knee in the face sobered Dana even as it infuriated him. He paused, swaying on his thick legs, his clawlike hands closing into fists.

Spitting the blood out of his mouth, he roared, "You've played your last belittlin' trick, Mistah Badly. I aim to break every bone in your body. You'll wish to hell my bullet had gone through your brain before I'm done with you!"

With that Dana came in cagily, his arms spread wide. Joel braced himself. Dana lunged, wrapped his big arms around Joel in a bear hug with a jerk that almost broke his back. Joel lost his wind. The big arms squeezed tighter, forcing his shoulders back and crushing his ribs. He kicked at Dana's shins, at the same time falling backward. Dana fell on top of him, but Dana's grip was broken.

Ignoring the pain of his crushed ribs, Joel slithered clear and staggered to his feet. Dana rose, sleeving the blood off his mouth. He mumbled curses under his breath. Joel knew he had to avoid those crushing arms. He weaved. Before Dana could get set for another charge, Joel darted in and smashed two blows to Dana's bloody face. He dodged to one side as Dana made a wild swing. The blow caught him on the side of the head and dazed him. He shook the haze out of his eyes and darted in, jabbing two more blows at Dana's head. A cut appeared over Dana's eye.

"Kick him in the guts, kid!" a man shouted. "He's been top bull long enough around here!"

Dutch Leiberg's voice rose above the noise. "Iff'n you want to die, hombre, keep bad-mouthin' Pete!"

To Joel the voices were a blur of sound. He was breathing hard, but Dana was breathing harder. From there on it was a battle of endurance. They traded blow for blow. Then Dana picked up a chair from one of the card tables. He raised it above Joel's weaving form.

Joel dodged as the chair came down, crashing on the floor. He charged Dana, driving a mighty blow to his chest that sent him sprawling across the card table to land on the other side. Two men pulled the card table out of the way, and the floor was clear all the way to the adobe wall. There was a hum of shouted remarks, some encouraging, some derisive. Joel didn't try to decipher them.

The news of the fight spread and men were coming in off the street. The bar girls were on one of the tables where they could get a better view.

One of the newcomers spoke encouragement in a level voice. "Run him to death, Joel. He don't have the wind for anything but gunplay." The voice sounded faintly familiar.

As the voice stopped, Joel took a blow to the solar plexus that gagged and winded him. He doubled up with the blow. Dana followed it with a knee to the face. Joel rolled to one side and lost his footing. Before he could get up, Dana's boot caught him in the neck. The impact of the pointed boot paralyzed him momentarily. He had to get up, he had to fight back or be kicked into unconsciousness. As Dana's boot came at him a second time, he managed to hook his arm around

Dana's ankle and drag his feet out from under him. They both got up, weaving and staggering. Joel spit the blood from his bruised mouth.

It was a fight to the hilt, maybe to the death. He looked at Dana's wobbly figure. He looked like a man with rubber legs. Drawing on his last dregs of strength, Joel moved in and caught Dana on his bloody jaw. Dana went crashing down at the base of the adobe wall. Then, in a red haze, Joel saw the gun that Dutch Leiberg had tossed at him and which he had dodged. It lay against the wall near Dana. Dana's hand groped for the gun. He steadied it with both hands. Joel's mind went blank. So this was to be the end! Fate intervened. A polished boot, hazed with dust, kicked the gun out of Dana's hand.

"No you don't, bigshot! You're nothing but a yellow-livered skunk!" the vaguely familiar voice exclaimed.

Dana, cursing, tried to rise, but he fell back unconscious. Joel, exhausted, fell to his knees and rolled over on his back. He couldn't see clearly. He heard the vaguely familiar voice. Men were paying off their wagers. Dutch Leiberg and Bull Dobel picked up Pete Dana and carried him away.

Joel blinked the blood and sweat out of his eyes. He had a vague vision of a man's face looking down at him and Lou Parker, one of the bar girls with her pretty face and silvery blonde hair, wiping the blood from his nose. Then he drifted into total darkness.

When Joel came to, he was on a bed, a soft bed with the feel of smooth sheets under him. He opened his eyes and took in the frilly trimmings of a vain woman's room. The lamplight cast a golden glow over the velvet chairs and lace curtains, and the coy fragrance of perfume scented the air. His head throbbed, but it was clear. His knuckles were sore and his joints stiff. He twisted his head and felt the sharp pain in his neck.

"Where am I? What happened?" he queried through swollen lips.

Meg Easter came to the bedside. She looked down at him with a half smile on her painted lips.

"You're in my room above the Vado Queen, Joel," she said. "You gave a good account of yourself. You put Pete Dana in his place. I'm not sure he'll stay there, but for tonight he'll know the misery he's been dealing out to others."

It all came back to Joel in a flash. "I—I don't feel so good myself, Meg. How did I get here?"

"You were carried here. This could have been the morgue if it wasn't for the interference of your cousin."

"My cousin?" He frowned. He thought of Margo and wondered how she had heard about the fight. "You—you mean *Margo* got mixed up in it?" There was disbelief in his voice.

Meg shook her head and brushed back her meticulously waved hair. "Not Margo."

Then a deeper voice came out of the shadows and a man looked down at him. "Have you forgotten me completely, Joel? Maybe you were a little young at the time of the squabble to understand it. But it wasn't that many years ago."

Joel was struck with wonder. His memory cleared and he gasped, "Why—why you're my cousin, Orson!"

"That's right, Joel, but now I've changed my name to Orson Miles."

"But—but nobody ever talks about you. Nobody knew or cared where you were. I wasn't sure what caused the fight between you and Uncle Earl. How come you turned up just at the right time to save my life and prevent Pete Dana from committing a murder?"

"One question at a time, cousin." Orson grinned. His straw-colored hair was combed neatly across his head. His broad shoulders were covered with a fine cashmere shirt, and his long legs were sheathed by serge California pants that were tucked into polished boots.

He continued. "First off, my father banished me because I married an Indian girl. White Feather was no ordinary Indian. She had been educated at the school in the Indian territory in Oklahoma. She had lived with the family of the superintendent of the school and had taught his children *indianismo*, the arts of Indian culture. She had come back to the Mescalero Reservation to share her learning with her tribesmen. I met her on a trip to Picacho."

"An' you mean you—you married her?" Joel asked, puzzled.

"Yes, I married her."

"By—by Indian custom?"

"Yes, at first. Since then we've been married by a padre in Santa Fe. Don't feel uneasy, Joel. I guess I'm a squaw-man in the literal sense of the word. Pa couldn't take it. Your uncle is reasonable and soft for about a half an inch under his skin, but then you hit hard rock. He wouldn't have anything more to do with me. As I said, don't fret yourself, cousin. Pa did me a favor by disowning me."

Joel noticed that Orson talked different from the way he or any of the other cowhands did. He talked like Emma Layton, the schoolteacher, and he was dressed better and was more self-assured. "What's it all about, Orson?"

"When Earl kicked me out, White Feather suggested that I go to school. She got me into the university they're starting at Alburquerque. That's when I changed my name. It didn't take me long to learn how to keep accounts, how to write official letters and meet important people. I was appointed by the Governor as an inspector of Indian affairs, with charge over the reservations and the schools.

"My job is to see that the supervisors of the reservations keep reasonably honest and that the kids are not cheated of the basics of education. It isn't an easy job. Some of the white men who take the job of running the reservations see it as an opportunity to line their pockets with the money meant to be used for the welfare of the Indians. White Feather goes with me. She's a sort of liaison between the Indians and me."

"What's that mean, liaison?"

"A connection, a sort of connecting link between the Indians and the whites. They trust her and through her they trust me. See what I mean, Joel?"

"I reckon I get your meanin', but I'm still fuddled how you got where you are. How come you just happen to be in Vado?"

"I've been traveling about. I even went to Washington once to report to the Bureau of Indian Affairs. When I heard you'd been sentenced to the federal prison in Yuma, along with your pa, I made it a point to come here and look into it. I could see your father getting into trouble with his hot temper, but I couldn't see you mixed up in a killing."

"It wasn't supposed to be a killing, Orson. I liked Jim Costly even though he couldn't get along with Pa. I was trying to save his life. You know how hotheaded my pa is. He claimed he wasn't going to shoot Jim, only knock the whip out of his hand. The Mexican laborers who were digging the postholes couldn't understand what the argument was about. They told just what they saw. They saw me push Costly and Pa shoot him."

"I know, I went into the testimony when I passed through Roswell on my way down here. I talked to Judge Cottle. He said he was inclined to believe you, but when the jury brought in a verdict of guilty, he had to abide by it. He gave you the lightest sentence he could. A lot of folks were expecting a hanging. Some were even recommending calling in *Judge Lynch*."

A thought struck Joel and he put it into words. "Were you the one who got my sentence cut short, Orson?"

"I might have been, except that Judge Cottle told me your sentence had already been commuted."

Joel felt a letdown. He was hoping Orson might have been the one to intercede on his behalf. There could still be somebody waiting around to rectify the verdict of the court. He put the thought into words.

"Somebody set me free, but I ain't sure if it was friend or foe. I figured tonight that Dana might have been paid to execute me. Lucky for me, you came along, Orson, or he might have succeeded."

"How's everything at the ranch, Joel?" Orson asked.

"Not good. Giles don't trust my brother, Sam. He's hired Pete Dana and his two pals to see that Sam don't cheat on the roundup."

"What about Margo? She must be quite a grown-up lady by now."

Joel debated whether to tell about his meeting with Margo at the creek. He looked around. Meg Easter had gone into the kitchen of her apartment. He motioned

Orson to lean close. Then he told the whole story of their meeting at the creek, a catch in his voice to betray his emotions.

Orson pulled his ear and said thoughtfully, "I suppose you were bound to feel that way, Joel."

"But it was so sudden. We were still pals when I left here, but I reckon when I saw Margo, so pure an' beautiful, something broke loose inside of me. I I fell in love with her. Of course, I've got to forget all that."

"You will, Joel. You will in time. And one day you'll meet the woman who's really meant for you. You'll know it right away, just as I knew it when I met Tonalea—that's the name White Feather uses when she's among white people."

Meg came in from the kitchen with Lou Parker, the silvery-blonde bar girl with a pretty face which would have been beautiful without the makeup that daubed it.

"Who washed the blood off my face and linimented my cuts?" Joel asked before they could speak.

"We both had a hand in it," Meg said.

"I ain't got no cause to ruffle your bed, Meg. I could have sobered up out in the alley."

"And have your head kicked in out in the alley, too," Lou said.

"I reckon that's true," Joel said soberly. He looked at Orson. "Git me my boots, cousin. I'll sleep with my horse in the livery barn. I got a *muchacho* friend down there watchin' over Volcan. It's time I spelled him." Joel swung his bare feet to the floor and realized he had no pants on. "Who undressed me?" he queried.

"We both had a hand in it," Lou Parker said, her vivid red lips smiling.

"They're teasing you, Joel," Orson said. "I undressed you. You were blood all the way down to your navel."

Orson helped him dress, and he talked as he did so. "I've got a room at the hotel, Joel. You can stay there for the night. The *muchacho* will make out."

Joel awoke in Orson's bed in the morning feeling stiff and sore but otherwise in fine fettle. He had fought Pete Dana to a draw, there was some satisfaction in that. There would be repercussions, he knew that. If Pete had been hired to kill him for a fee, he wouldn't give up easily.

Orson, pulling on his boots on the opposite side of the bed, spoke up.

"Are you going to keep running around without a gun, cousin?"

"I reckon a gun is an invitation to a gunfight, Orson."

"Are you afraid of a gunfight, Joel?"

"What are you doin', cousin, tryin' me out? I reckon I can draw as fast as most, and shoot as straight, but I ain't usin' my gun to win a reputation that will dog me at every turn of the road. Supposin' I had killed Dana last night? That would make the other men edgy toward me. I'd be known as the man who killed Dana, the head bull, and I'd inherit his place."

"And if Dana had killed you, you'd be dead, cousin," Orson said grimly. "You'd be known, or remembered, as that brash kid from the BB who bit off more than he could swallow."

"Do you carry a gun, Orson?" Joel asked.

"Yes." Orson pointed at the shoulder holster

hanging under his coat on a chair. "Come on, let's get some breakfast."

"Where's Tonalea?" Joel asked while he wiped his wet face and inspected it in the foggy mirror.

"She's at the reservation. The Jicarilla's close by. I have a job there checking the accounts."

"Livin' like the Indians?"

"Living *with* the Indians. She wins their trust and through her, they trust me. Get a move on, I'm starved."

Conchita's Cafe was part of the Vado Hotel. They had slept overtime and now the neat eatery was almost empty, but the spicy smell of frying ham and steaming coffee still lingered in the place. They took a table near the window where they could watch the street. Conchita bustled toward them, her ample hips squirming like two bear cubs in a blanket.

"You late," she admonished. "You got some beeg-shot job, eh?" she said to Orson, admiring his cashmere shirt and spotless sombrero lying on the chair next to him.

"Big enough to keep me in *frijoles* and *cerveza*, Conchita."

She turned her attention to Joel, frowning at his cut and bruised face. "I theenk maybe you have too much *cerveza* last night, *senor*. What hoppen? You look like *el toro* put the horns and also a foot on top of your face."

"It wasn't any bullfight, Conchita, just a little misunderstanding." Joel smiled, feeling his cuts and bruises in the process.

"I theenk maybe someone is standing on your face,

Senor Joel. What you like for eat thees late morning?"

"What have you got left, *senora?*"

"*Bistec, jamon, huevos,* and *cafe.*"

"Just bring us ham and eggs, plenty of coffee," Orson told her.

They were halfway through the meal when Joel, looking out the window, said in a tight voice, "Pete Dana is headin' this way alone, cousin. His face don't look no better'n mine."

"Is he armed?"

"I reckon he sleeps with his iron on."

"Let him make the first move," Orson cautioned, patting the bulge in his coat that concealed his holster.

"I reckon he's not too happy," Joel mused. He was still without a gun.

"Perhaps he learned a lesson last night," Orson suggested.

There was no time for cogitation. Dana came in the door, his warped hat on the back of his tousled black hair. He came over directly to Joel with no sign of belligerence. He even attempted a wry smile. One eye was discolored and his face was slightly puffed in places.

"Mornin', men," he said in a conciliatory tone. "I seen you through the window. I had a long night to think things over. I'm sorry about the ruckus last night, Badly. Too much booze, Meg eggin' me on, an' the way you stood up to me, threw me off balance. You downed me, Badly, an' I ain't been down before."

Joel, taken by surprise at Dana eating humble pie, decided on a little magnanimity on his part. "I'd call that fight a draw, Dana. You just happened to fall down first. I wasn't long in followin' your example. Why the sudden peace pipe?"

"I reckon it might seem a mite peculiar, Badly, but I ain't slittin' my wrist to make you a blood brother. We're headin' out on a roundup in a couple of days. No roundup can prosper if they's contention an' bad blood in the outfit. You can call this a temporary peace if you like an' when things settle down, we can try each other with guns, knives, fists, or name-callin'. Who knows? By the time the dogies is counted an' branded, we might become bosom friends."

Joel grinned wryly. "I ain't gonna swear off likker until that happens, but I'll shake on it."

The two men shook hands in the manner of the West. A handshake was as good as a gold seal.

Orson ran a hand across his neat, straw-colored hair, and there was amusement in his brown eyes. "As the Good Book says, the lion shall lie down with the lamb. The only catch is to find out which is which." He added, "Sit down, Dana, and have a cup of coffee with us."

After the strange meeting they left the cafe, each going about his business. Men and even some women loitering on the boardwalk eyed them warily. The fight of the night before had become common knowledge, and the sight of the two adversaries apparently on friendly terms puzzled them.

"Orson, I reckon I'll stick around town until the stage comes in, so I can pick up the mail," Joel said.

"I've got business out at the reservation," Orson told him. "White Feather will be wondering what happened to me."

When Orson had gone, Joel moseyed toward the stage depot. He passed Dutch Leiberg and Bull Dobel on the way. He stiffened as they went by, but they waved their hands in greeting and moved on. To Joel, things began to look a little fishy.

CHAPTER SIX

Joel stepped into the stage depot, mulling over in his mind the strange turn of events. He greeted the agent who was busy getting freight and mail lined up to put on the stage. The stage line ran from El Paso in Texas, north through Santa Fe, and ended in Denver where the new branch line of the railroad from Cheyenne had been completed. Joel passed the time by studying the *wanted* posters adorning the walls and wondered what it would be like to turn bounty hunter and track down some of the culprits.

Near noon he heard the rattle of the stage coming down the road. Instead of going out into the hot sun, he waited inside the cool adobe building for the mail to be brought in. There was the usual bustle when the stage stopped and the horses were changed. The passengers, taking advantage of the delay, had decided to eat some lunch. He studied the half-dozen passengers as they came through the door, four men and two women. Then he tensed and a lump came into his throat. On the heels of the other six passengers came Margo Giles and her mother!

Unnerved by the confrontation, Joel restrained himself. He had relegated Margo to the back of his mind knowing how hopeless was his desire for her. But the sight of her, dressed in a trim, gray traveling suit, her golden hair under her pert little hat framing her soft face with its red lips and deep blue eyes, shattered his emotions. She spied him and there was no escape. Her honest face slightly flushed, she came directly toward him, her chin up.

"Why, Joel, how fortunate to find you here!" she exclaimed.

Joel swallowed hard as he read in her face the love she was bravely concealing.

"I—I stayed over to pick up the mail," he said huskily. "I had no idea you would be leaving so suddenly."

"Mother thought it best to get rid of me before the start of the roundup for fear I'd stow away in the chuck wagon," she said pertly.

"I'm not getting *rid* of you, Margo. You're being spiteful. I want to spare you the heartbreak you would have to endure if you remained at the ranch," Elsa said frankly. "I'm doing this for both of you. You understand that, don't you, Joel?"

"I'm not sure the separation will change my feelings, Elsa. It might just deepen them," Joel said.

"Not if I become a nun," Margo said with a touch of defiance.

"Stop talking like that!" Elsa scolded. "You'll each find someone new. I know that from my own experience."

"Are you making a confession, Mother? I never suspected you of having so much experience," Margo said.

Elsa looked away. "Call it a confession if you wish. I shan't unburden my past to amuse you. People are watching—edging close to hear what we say. You had better check your suitcase, honey."

"Is this all you're taking?" Joel asked, picking up the modest portmanteau.

"She can shop when she gets there and buy clothes approved by the nuns, which will be more suitable for the climate," Elsa explained.

The moment Joel dreaded was soon upon them, the moment of good-bye. He didn't trust himself to embrace Margo. There was a deadly finality about this parting that would haunt him for days to come. Margo was braver than he. She faced him with a determination that bordered on defiance.

"Aren't you going to kiss your cousin good-bye?" she asked, lifting her face toward him.

Joel wanted to change the subject by telling her about Orson being in town, but he deferred the thought, not sure that Orson wanted the fact known. He had a hunch that was one reason Orson had left for the reservation. Then, somewhat surprised that she had not commented on the still-visible signs on his face left there by Dana's fists, he got another idea.

"You wouldn't want to kiss a battered mug like

mine, would you? I had a slight misunderstanding with Dana last night."

"I heard about the fight before we reached town. Jess Slater of the Pot-Hook, told us about it on his way home from town. I hope you weren't fighting over that kiss Dana forced on me."

"I reckon the fight started over the fact that I was out of jail so soon, but the memory of that stolen kiss might have had something to do with the outcome," he explained with a touch of gallantry.

She smiled, whimsy in her blue eyes. "I'm giving kisses away today, cousin. I saved one of them for you. You'd better take it, it might be your last."

The thought of not holding her and kissing her ever again was suffocating. He succumbed to her bold offer, making sure to keep the kiss light.

Elsa came between them.

"Break it off, you two. People are beginning to stare," she told them.

Joel released Margo, avoiding her eyes. He put on his tall hat, pulling the brim down over his face as he walked from the busy stage office without looking back. It was over. It was done. It should never have been.

He walked to the livery barn, forgetting the mail he had intended to pick up. To hell with the mail. He was glad the roundup was only a couple of days off. It would clear his mind of the folly that had beset him. With the motley crews Earl Giles and his brother Sam Badly had hired, there would be few dull moments.

As he entered the barn, he thought of Porferio. He had forgotten the *muchacho* in the excitement of the night before. He expected to find the Mexican boy gone to spend the dollar he had paid him in advance. To his dismay and amusement, he found Porferio nodding on a pile of bedding straw.

"So you're still here, *muchacho*," Joel greeted him.

"*Seguro, senor*. The *caballerizo*, the groom, he get dronk. I geeve the *caballo agua* to dreenk, and the *heno* to eat."

"So you watered and fed my horse, but did you feed yourself?"

"I am not hongry, *senor*. I eat weeth the horse some oats. I tell you I watch for the horse. I am wan honest hombre, *senor*."

"Porferio, you are a *caballero*, a gentleman. Here's two pesos for your loyalty," Joel said, handing him two additional dollars. "Go fill your belly. The next time I come to Vado, I'll look you up."

Back home, Joel threw himself into the work of getting outfitted for the roundup. The wagons were greased and repaired where necessary, and the water barrels were soaked up watertight. There were the three steady hands on the crew, Tom Crawley, Archy Trable, and Herb Sontag, and they accepted Joel back as though he had never been in prison.

The two new hands Sam had hired were edgy men who looked on him with subdued suspicion. Their names were Mike Stiller and Jag Oby. Stiller had a mean cast to his features, but he spoke softly and to the point. Jag Oby was a swarthy man with a hint of Indian in him, or Mexican. They left no doubt as to their calling. Drovers, yes, but with additional accomplishments they made no effort to disguise.

Their guns were tied low on their legs, and Oby's gun

bore five notches. The notches could mean little or nothing. A man who advertised his score was usually a braggart. Joel felt that Stiller was the man to watch out for.

Joel brought it up to Sam while they were checking over the harness and riding gear in the barn.

"How come, Sam, you hired Oby and Stiller? Are you expectin' trouble?"

"I hired 'em to keep trouble from startin', Joel."

"To me they look like men itchin' to find trouble so they can have the fun of puttin' it down."

"Uncle Giles hired Pete Dana and his sidekicks for a reason. He figgers I'm holdin' a grudge against him for callin' the law on you an' Pa, an' makin' you stand trial when Jim Costly's death could have been passed off as an accident. The trial was rigged with them Mexican witnesses. Pa didn't get to be top dog on the Tularosa Range without makin' enemies.

"They figure you an' Pa should have been sentenced to hang. They're grumbling 'cause you're out of jail early. That was what started the fight twixt you an' Dana in the Vado Queen accordin' to what I've heard. We can't take that kind of pushin' around without retaliation. You won the fight, but Dana won't take that beating lying down."

"Nobody won. It was a draw. And Dana has called a truce until after the roundup," Joel explained.

"Any truce Dana called will be like that of a rattlesnake waiting for the proper moment to strike."

"Have you any idea who spoke the word that got my sentence cut short?"

"I ain't got no notion, Joel. You must have a friend who wants to evade trouble."

"Or an enemy who wants to make trouble for me, Sam. Ma suggested that somebody pried me loose from Yuma so they could kill me. Not everybody agreed with Judge Cottle's sentence. When Dana tried to force me into a shootout, I figgered he might be the man, or have been hired by the real man behind my release," Joel explained.

"You said that Dana called a truce," Sam reminded him.

"Until after the roundup," Joel prompted.

"You know you could get killed accidental-like on the range, brother."

"What do you expect me to do, Sam, crawl out of the country?"

"No. If anybody's serious about executin' you, they could follow you no matter where you go. My advice is to wear a gun. You an' Margo done pretty good outdrawin' each other. Fast, sure, but shootin' at a man is a different proposition. As you know, I've only killed one man, an' he was a rustler who shot at me first."

"I ain't out to make a rep as a killer, Sam, but I aim to wear a gun, carry a rifle in the boot on my saddle, an' have a sheath-knife danglin' on my belt," Joel said grimly.

The roundup started the following day with a meeting of all hands to decide on how and where each group would function. The Box-G had their own chuck wagon and supply buckboard. That was a distrustful arrangement in the very beginning, but Joel and Sam didn't question it. Giles was ramrodding his own crew which consisted of his three regular hands, Kiler, Fibbs, and Rasco, and his hired bonus crew of Dana, Leiberg, and Dobel. The BB, ramrodded by Sam

Badly, with Joel as his segundo, had three regulars, Crawley, Trable, and Sontag, to which were added Mike Stiller and Jag Oby. Pop Keller came along as cook on the chuck wagon, and had a rawboned lad as flunky. His name was Josiah, but the men called him *Shuffle* because of his walk.

"Uncle Giles," Sam said, opening the meeting, "with Pa gone, me an' Joel is goin' to run our end of the roundup. You can discuss whatever comes up with either or both of us."

"Aren't you forgetting one thing, Sam?" Giles interposed.

"What's that?"

"Joel is a felon. His release don't change that. He has no jurisdiction over property. That's the law," Giles pointed out.

"How come you're so sure of that, Uncle Earl? Do you know the terms of my release? I might have got a full pardon from the Governor, restorin' my right of franchise. I aim to look into that. I'll argue my rights and standing when the time comes."

Pete Dana, hoping to take the edge off his humiliation in the Vado Queen, said with a touch of humor, "Don't git into fisticuffs with Joel Badly. There ain't no way to handle him proper. He's gun-shy, but he fights like a female wolf with a batch of puppies. I ain't done with him. You're all invited to a showdown fight when the roundup is over."

"My status has nothin' to do with the roundup. I aim to do my share of the work and expect no favors," Joel said.

They discussed the details of the roundup, dividing the range into sections. The rougher riding in the big thicket was split up between the two outfits. The men chose buddies to ride with, and each outfit had a representative from the other to keep a tab on things.

Sam drew Joel aside. "You ride with Uncle Earl's cavvy, Joel. I ain't sure what Earl has up his sleeve, but he's actin' sort of peculiar, just like callin' you a felon. I'll admit things were getting sticky between Pa and Earl before Pa shot Jim Costly. With Pa gone our uncle might fancy hisself top dog. I aim to see that he's not."

"I ain't sure I relish spyin' on Earl, Sam. He distrusts me because I'm a Badly. I figger he distrusts our whole outfit. You know, I never thought things would get this bad between our outfit and Uncle Earl's. Only bad can come of it—all this distrust from Uncle Earl."

"Well, I don't feel trustful toward Earl myself, Joel. He's a changed man. Jim's death sure brought his meanness to the surface. I reckon playin' second fiddle to Pa all these years has galled him. He aims to get some kind of revenge for all those years, while Pa's away in Yuma Prison. I ain't goin' to let him hornswaggle us, Joel. He hired Pete Dana an' his pals for a purpose. Either he figures I aim to get the bigger cut of the herd, or he aims to get it for hisself."

"How can he do that, Sam?"

"He can hide some of the cattle in the thicket. There's places there that are hard to get to. After the roundup is over, he'll bring a crew out to gather those cattle an' brand 'em Box-G. That's where Dana and his men come in. They'll back the play with their guns if it comes to that."

"I still feel squeamish spyin' on Earl. Why don't you send Herb Sontag over there as our rep. He's been with us for three years. He's tough and honest as far as I know," Joel suggested.

"Mebbe you're right, Joel," Sam said. "We'll pick up

the reps of the three smaller ranches and let one of 'em ride with Earl along with Sontag."

The two outfits took off toward Tularosa Valley, one some distance behind the other to avoid the dust. They kept formation until they reached the open range and then spread apart a few hundred feet more or less flanking the area on which the branding of the cattle and the castrating of the young bulls would take place. The castrated bull calves would grow into meaty steers, the most prized merchandise at the stock auctions.

The chuck wagons had gone on ahead and now the supply wagons carrying the men's extra gear and bedrolls stopped near them. The remuda made up of the spare horses, of which there were four for each man, was shunted off near the stream of water that ran near the branding grounds, with a cowboy to see that the horses didn't stray too far.

Joel had always savored the excitement of the roundup, and this time the excitement was heightened by the tension between the two camps. He remembered his first roundup when he was only ten years old. The herd had not been so large then, and the feeling between his father and his half-brother had been friendly and cooperative. Jim Costly had taken him under his wing, and had taught him the routine and fine points of branding and castration. His impression on that first roundup was that the branding and the castrating were cruel, but he soon learned how necessary they were. Now he was inured to both operations, and he faced his job with determination tinged with vague misgivings.

It was twilight when the men were finished rubbing down their mounts and turning them in with the rest of the remuda. Shuffle, who had driven the supply wagon, was now helping Pop Keller over the camp stove, his face beaded with sweat. The men, tapping their tin cups against their tin plates, were joshing among themselves, and good-natured epithets were sprinkled generously through their joshing.

"Hey, Pop, ain't you never goin' to get that chow on the line? My stomach is stuck to my damned backbone!" Tom Crawley called out.

Pop's retort was, "You go to hell, Crawley! I'm gittin' this chuck out jest as fast as the good Lord'll cook it. This damned firewood ain't particular dry, an' I ain't had nobody to rustle up some withered mesquite stumps."

The food was eventually served and the men sat on the ground wolfing it down. Spirits were high, but the hard work of the following days would dampen them, and after a week the healthy griping would begin. But now there was still more joshing than griping.

Joel lay under the stars, which, on the high desert, were like brilliant jewels within reach of plucking fingers. His saddle under his head, his boots by his side, and his gun within the fold of his blanket, he wooed sleep, but sleep was slow in coming. His mind was haunted with visions of Margo: her soft lips, her blue eyes, and the clean smell of her pale golden hair. His love for her was as intense as pain, and the fact that she was unreachable only heightened his emotions.

By now she would be halfway to Santa Fe, that ancient city, with its Mission San Miguel defying the elements of that high plateau for over two hundred years. He wondered if the nuns at the convent could squelch her love of the open range and instill in her the proprieties that would fit her into the parlors and drawing rooms of the rich or famous. The man who won her would be the envy of his friends, and the wives would be envious and aloof toward her. Finally, exhaustion from the strenuous labors of the day brought sleep that released him from his mental torture.

The following day was clear and tempered by the September breeze that took the edge off the heat. The men were up before sunrise and when the breakfast of side meat, hot cakes, and pungent coffee was over, Dusty Kiler, lean and gray with the eyes of an eagle, came over from Giles's camp.

"Earl figgers I should ride with you fellers," Kiler said, shaking the ash off his quirlie.

Sam retorted in an edgy voice, "What's the matter? Is he afraid I'll steal him blind?"

"Don't lay it on me, Sam," Kiler said in a quiet voice. "I'm jest takin' orders. I know one thing. Giles intends to git his share of the cattle come hell or high water. He's offerin' each man a dollar a head bonus fer every cow they swing his way."

"That sounds downright dishonest to me, Kiler, but two can play at the same game. I'm sendin' Herb Sontag over to ride with Earl's crew. If Giles figures he can do as he pleases while Pa's in jail, he'd better think again. I'm aimin' to make an honest tally an' expect the same thing of him. Giles is askin' for an equal split once the tally is made. He ain't takin' into account that Pa was the one with the guts to fight the Apache to win the range, and that Pa weeded out the rustlers, damned near gittin' exterminated twice for his efforts. Giles was always the tagalong, but Pa treated him fair. Giles, spiteful because he resented Pa's domination, called on the law in the Jim Costly killin'. It could have been handled local like other shootouts, but Giles was eager to see Pa go to the federal prison at Yuma."

"You cain't fault Giles fer callin' in the law," Kiler objected. "We gotta live by the law here someday and it was a good place to start."

"Well, I'm sendin' over my man, Herb Sontag, to see that Earl lives by the law hisself," Sam warned.

Joel, hearing the last part of the conversation, rode over. "I reckon, if you agree, Sam, that I'll play the part of range sleuth on our side. Most of the talk I'm hearin' ain't exactly friendly. If Uncle Earl wants half the cattle, you can't very well short him. Him an' Pa was partners for years."

"I just aim to see he doesn't get more'n his share," Sam said flatly.

The roundup proceeded with a flourish as the men caught up their half-wild ponies and mounted. Sontag, himself branded with a knife scar on his face, rode over to Giles's camp. Stiller and Oby elected to ride together. Sam gave Joel his choice of Crawley or Trable. Joel picked Trable, a short, stocky man, but one with a sense of humor. So the riders scattered in several directions.

CHAPTER SEVEN

Joel and Trable took off toward Expectro Peak, so named because the white chalky limestone traced white lines among the mesquite and sagebrush like the bones of a skeleton. The early rains had coaxed a fuzz of green grass from the rocky sand of the desert. Giant saguaros stood along the way like sentinels with upthrust arms, whispering to themselves as the wind swirled within the cluster of their limbs.

Trable, slouched in the saddle as his pony ambled through the twisted barriers of mesquite, spat out his cud of tobacco and opined, "They's somethin' spooky about this roundup, Badly. When your pa was here we allus traveled in one big cavvy, eatin' the same chuck, tradin' lookouts, an' hurrahin' each other when we got

81

throwed or gored. Now we're two camps, each with its own gunsharps an' ramrods. It appears t'me like a troublesome arrangement."

Joel, straight in the saddle on Volcan's back, said, "There may be trouble, Arch. I reckon I'm part of the trouble already. You've heard about my fight with Pete Dana, ain't you?"

"Hell, everybody's heard about it. You should've tromped him into his grave whilst you was at it. Might've saved a heap of trouble."

"I didn't have the strength left to tromp a mouse, Arch. I figure the fight was more of a draw than anything else."

"It wouldn't have been no draw if that stranger hadn't kicked the gun outta Dana's hand."

"Did anybody say anything about the stranger, Arch?"

"Only that he was a dude in fancy duds with a hideout gun in a shoulder holster. He had guts, though. There ain't many dudes who would have horned in on Pete Dana when he was in a mood fer slaughter. If it hadn't been fer the stranger, you would be dead an' Dana would have been rope bait. I reckon that would've been some kind of a draw, at that."

Joel had a notion to speak Orson's name, but he squelched it. Few people would recognize Orson now as the spunky, hair-chaps cowboy who married a squaw against his father's wishes. Orson could make himself known when the time pleased him.

"That fight isn't over yet, Arch. Dana practically apologized."

"That don't sound like Pete Dana. He never apologized to nobody, especially to a ranny who knocked him cold."

"He promised me a rematch after the roundup, Arch. I think he's got some scheme brewin' which he don't want to spoil. He's bidin' his time. I have a hunch he means to corner me into a shootout after the roundup an' kill me."

"Hey, they's a bunch of dogies grazin near the salt licks near them low hills," Trable said, pointing with his gloved hand.

"Let's get around 'em and head 'em back toward the brandin' grounds," Joel said.

They split up, one going to the left and the other to the right. Joel hazed the scattered cattle together with a wave of his hat and a few well-chosen epithets. Volcan knew what was expected of him and swung out after the stubborn half-grown calves who had not yet experienced a roundup. They got the twenty head started back toward the camp and rode on toward the higher rugged cone of Expectro Peak.

North of the peak in a shallow canyon called Dead Horse Pass was a water hole fed by a spring that spilled from the rock. They headed that way, taking note of the scattered cattle they would pick up on their way back. The water hole was in a basin of red rock and surrounded by aspen and chokecherry bushes, their green leaves tinged with the gold of autumn. Cattle were lying in the shade of the trees to escape the heat of the noonday sun. Broken spires of red rock were thrust up near the side of the water.

"Might as well take a noon break here, Arch," Joel suggested. "The water's cold an' pure. I reckon we'll ride to the other side of the peak, an' then head back with what dogies we can pick up. There's grass hereabouts for the horses to browse."

They unsaddled their mounts, scrubbed off the

sweat with handsful of grass, and turned them loose.
Then they washed off the dust of the morning's ride in
the cold water and raked back their hair with their
fingers.

"This is a right purty spot, Badly," Arch opined,
looking about.

"There used to be a Comanchero camp here years
ago, Arch. Comancheros are the scum of the earth.
They'd kill their own brother for a sack of Bull
Durham. They robbed the wagon trains hereabouts an'
the stagecoaches, killin' anybody who didn't fork over
their last peso. The army finally chased them across the
border into Mexico, but they still sneak back to steal
cattle, money, or women."

"I had a run-in with 'em once. They attacked and
killed a woman I loved. I reckon I went a little loco that
day. And I shot the guys who did it. I was gonna marry
that gal. I'll never forget that day, not as long as I—"

Trable's words were interrupted by the sudden crack
of a rifle. Joel, the canteen to his lips, felt the steel bottle
torn from his hands. Instinctively he dived behind a
fallen tree. Trable was crawling toward his rifle in the
boot on his saddle. Joel lay half stunned by the sudden
attack. He searched the skyline but saw nothing.

"Where did that shot come from?" Trable asked,
levering a cartridge into the firing chamber of his rifle.

Joel was studying the red spires above the north
bank of the pond. "I ain't sure. The canteen kept the
bullet from hittin' my head an' saved my life. The
smack of the bullet came before the sound of the rifle,
so the killer can't be too close."

"Do you reckon it's a renegade Apache off the
Mescalero?" Trable asked.

"A lone Apache wouldn't leave the reservation. This

log ain't no protection, Arch. Let's snake over to the crevice between that broken ledge at the base of the embankment. The echoes from that shot was a mite confusin'."

They reached the crevice without incident and flattened themselves between the ridges of rock.

"If it ain't no Indian, who the hell is it?"

"Mebbe a Comanchero come back for a look at the old campgrounds," Joel suggested. "Maybe a friend of the ones you shot."

"If he recognizes me," Trable said, "he'll be out for revenge."

"Mebbe it's me somebody's shooting at," Joel told him.

"I thought you said Dana had called a truce until after the roundup."

"There could be somebody else after me, Arch. I ain't got no notion who sprung me outta prison. At first I thought it was a friend who figured I had got a bum deal at the trial over Jim Costly's death. Then my ma warned me it might be an enemy who figured I got off too easy and wanted me out for an execution."

"Badly, you are in a chancy fix. Still, I reckon maybe the killer shot an' made a run for it. When the bullet hit the canteen, an' you dived for the log, he might have figgered you were dead. Anyhow, we can't stay here all day. Let's skirmish around for a sign. At least we can tell if it was a moccasin or a boot."

"You take the broken red cliff. There you can find cover in the rocks. I aim to climb to the top of Expectro an' have a look-see at the surrounding country. The backshooter can't be far off. He's either hidin' close by, or he's hightailin' it across the open country."

"I reckon you'll make a fine target climbin' the

peak," Trable warned. His square face was solemn and the usual twinkle was gone from his dark eyes. "I ain't partial to havin' my pardner kilt whilst he's on patrol with me."

"There's cover on the hill, an' it ain't very high," Joel assured him.

Joel knew that climbing the peak in cowboy boots would be no picnic, but if he got part way up, he could scan the country. His rifle in one hand and his .44 caliber single-action Colt tied to his leg, he crawled across the open space to the green fringe of chaparral that bordered the pond. Once there, he straightened up and threaded his way through the brush and stunted junipers to the base of the peak.

He emerged from the chaparral and climbed warily part way up the side of the mountain that was scarred and gouged by a million years of erosion. Pausing to get his breath, he looked around. He could see for some distance to the north and west across the mesquite and saguaro-studded landscape, but he picked out no sign of a rider among the shadows of the desert foliage. He proceeded higher up the peak, taking advantage of the gullies and potholes carved out by the force of wind and cloudbursts. He reached a saddle near the top of the peak which afforded him a wide view of the country.

He sat down easing his feet which were already chafing from the tight, high-heeled boots that were made for a stirrup and not for rocks and shale. Shading his eyes, he noticed a ribbon of dust far to the north. He studied the ribbon of dust, thinking it might be some of his Uncle Earl's men heading a bunch of cows toward the roundup camp. He was puzzled to discover that the dust-cloud wasn't going toward the camp, but away from it. It was headed toward that dark, tangled area of tall brush and stunted trees known as The Thicket.

Only the wildest cattle braved The Thicket with its thorny bushes and spiny cactus. He watched the ribbon of dust until it disappeared behind a tall mesa that stood out purple and black from that distance. He decided that the men causing the dust must be some of the riders consolidating a real large bunch of cattle to bring in for branding and whatever.

From the saddle where he sat, a gray wall rose up to the top of Expectro. It was a rugged wall, chiseled with steps marking the strata of rock laid down patiently by millions of years of rugged sculpturing by the builder of the earth. He decided to scale the cliff instead of going around it. The cliff was not perpendicular, but receded back step by step so the going was slow but not strenuous. He was halfway up the cliff, like a fly clinging to a wall, when the smash of a bullet, splintering the rock beside him, and the report of a rifle came simultaneously!

He froze against the rock. He was a clay pigeon in a shooting gallery. He searched for a crevice or a clump of greasewood that would give him cover. The sound of the shot had come from above him. He thought of the rifle, slung across his back. Even if he could bring it to bear, there was nothing to shoot at. Another bullet fingered the high crown of his hat and he cursed out loud.

In desperation he lay down prone on the ledge of rock on which he stood. Another bullet smashed into the rock below him. He realized the man must not be above him, but to one side. Or else there were two men. There was another bulkier ledge parallel to the one he was trapped on. The killer could be there, placing his bullets with precise care.

Joel managed to slip the strap of his rifle off his shoulder and swing the gun around to a prone firing position. He kept his eyes riveted on the opposite cliff. There was the flash of sunlight on steel, and he fired a shot at it. There was an answering shot that clipped the rock under his body. Whoever was shooting was a lousy shot. Any man worth his salt could shoot better than that. He thought of Indians. They were poor shots, firing mostly from running horses or without allowing for windage or trajectory.

Then a rifle barked from down below, near the pond. Trable was diverting the killer's attention! Joel looked down over the edge of the ledge on which he lay, and saw Trable scrambling up the opposite cliff.

Joel yelled, "Watch yourself, Arch! The killer's in them crannies someplace!"

"Cover me, Badly!" Trable yelled back.

Joel got to his knees, levering a new charge into the firing chamber of his carbine. He waited expectantly for the ambusher to show himself, but no one appeared. When Trable reached a point opposite him where he had seen the flash of sunlight on steel, he yelled, "That's where the ranny was hid out, Arch! Do you see any tracks?"

"The danged rock's too hard for tracks, Badly. I see somethin' else, though. Right here in this clump of bushes. There's a hole goin' back into the mountain. Looks like somebody dug a tunnel here!"

"Stay there, Arch. I'll make my way over to you!"

Joel edged around the side of the cliff he was on and came to a swale between the cliffs that was choked with mesquite, rock maple, and aspen. He worked his way through the thick growth until he came out on the opposite ledge where Arch awaited him.

"I tole you you'd make a fine target climbin' the peak, Joel," Arch scolded him.

"But I wasn't picked off, Arch. I got to thinkin' that mebbe the hombre didn't aim to kill me—just put the fear of God in me."

"I don't get it, Joel. Whyfor would a man waste bullets in a game of cat an' mouse?"

"That's just what he's doin', Arch, playin' cat an' mouse. He aims to let me live in misery and suspense until he's ready to finish the execution."

"That's a right unpleasant thought, Badly. I ain't got much recollect of the trial. You an' your pa didn't really gang up on Costly, did you?"

"In the name of God, no!" Joel objected vociferously. "I liked Jim Costly, he was always friendly to me. Costly an' my pa had their differences, but I could not figure out what they were. Somehow I gotta figure out the name of the person who got me released. I ain't got no notion who it might be or why they don't want to be known."

"Well, we cain't go fiddlin' around here. We gotta bring the cows to camp afore nightfall," Trable remarked.

"I want to look in this hole you're talkin' about, Arch. The hombre who was throwin' lead my way musta gone into the hole."

Joel parted the bushes and there was a hole there big enough for a man to walk through hunched over.

"I just thought of something," Joel mused. "Years

ago, when I was a kid there was rumors about Indian gold in Expectro Peak. There was a minor gold rush. Several accidents happened on the peak. A man was blowed up by his own powder. Another man was killed by a rattlesnake. It was rumored that the peak was haunted by the spirits of dead Indians. Finally, the hunt for gold was given up when two prospectors drilled a tunnel right through the peak an' found nothin'. The peak ain't very wide up here. Stick your head in the hole, Arch. You can feel a draft of air comin' through."

Arch complied and frowned. "It's air, all right, an' it smells fresh. Do you reckon the bushwacker came through the tunnel to spy on us, leavin' his hoss on the other side?"

"That's just what I do reckon. Somebody saw us ride out from camp an' seen us head for the pond. They climbed the other side of the peak, came through the tunnel, leavin' their horse on the other side, like you said."

"Do you think it could be one of the men who dug the tunnel?"

"No, Arch, it couldn't be one of them. They was old prospectors when they dug the hole. I'm sure they're dead an' buried now, just like the memory of the gold rush. Somebody ran across this tunnel accidental an' remembered it. As you say, we ain't got no time to stand here an' speculate. If the backshooter is someone who wants to devil me, he'll keep up his shenanigans. In the meantime we'd better get them cows gathered an' herded back to camp."

They reached the roundup camp when the sun was

sinking behind the San Andreas Mountains in the west. The other men were already in with their gather and were filling out tally sheets. Joel told Arch not to mention the shooting.

Giles, who was comparing figures with Sam Badly, gave Joel a sharp look. "You're the last one in, Joel. Have any trouble?"

"Just the ordinary. We found some dogies at the salt licks, bunched 'em, an' sent them driftin' toward camp. We went on to the Expectro water hole, an' found cattle restin' in the shade. We ate lunch there an' gave our horses a breather. There was some coyotes there sizin' up the yearlings. I killed one of 'em an' scared the others off." The last part was a pure fabrication. He waited for Giles's reaction.

"Did you save the pelts from the coyotes?"

"Naw, they wasn't furred out yet. They're just startin' to make their winter coat. I took the time to climb up Expectro an' get a look at the surrounding country, figgerin' I might spot some cattle close enough to run in with our herd."

"Did you see any over that way?" Sam broke in.

"Not close in. I could see all the way up to the purple mesa. Who was ridin' in that direction?"

"Pete Dana, Jesse Slater of the Pot-Hook, and Stiller," Sam said.

"They must've brung in a sizeable bunch," Joel hazarded.

"What makes you say that, Joel?" Sam asked. "They brought in a few more'n you did, that's all."

Joel pushed back his sorrel hair and scratched his ear. "From the looks of the dust cloud they was makin'

I figured it was a hundred head at least. They was headed around the end of the mesa toward the thicket. I lost sight of them after that."

Giles said quickly, "How the hell are you going to count cattle at a distance of several miles?"

"Mebbe the dust was extra thick," Joel said flatly.

When the cattle were bedded down for the night, Giles and his crew headed back to their camp for chuck. When they were gone Sam turned to Joel.

"You made a kinda skeptical statement in front of Giles," he admonished.

"I was hopin' to get some reaction from him, Sam."

"You got a reaction, all right. It sounded like you was accusing him of not bringin' in all the cattle they gathered. Things is touchy enough around here. Sontag didn't report anything out of line."

"Who did Sontag come in with?"

"He come in with Earl, Rasco, an' Bull Dobel."

"That left Pete Dana, Jesse Slater, an' Stiller."

"I told you they came in from the north," Sam repeated.

"How much tally did we make today, Sam?"

"Three hundred an' seventy. The first gather is always short. We'll have to move farther out on the high desert before we pick up any sizeable count. It ain't too short, though."

"How many do you figger we'll gather?"

"Last spring we rounded up over five thousand head. We sold three hundred head to the Mescalero and Pueblo Indian Reservations. After that I threw in with Chisum's trail herd, took a thousand head to Dodge. The price at the time we reached Dodge was purty solid."

"How much kickback did you pay the superintendents of the reservations?" Joel asked, thinking of Orson.

"The supers are cagey these days, they didn't ask for no kickback."

"That's always been one of the fringe benefits for holdin' down the thankless job," Joel prodded.

"Right now there ain't no fringe benefits, Joel. The supers make it on their salaries or what they can cheat the Indians out of on pelts. Seems like there's a new rovin' inspector policin' the reservations, demanding strictly honest accounts. He's some college man, I've heard."

Joel wanted to blurt out Orson's name, but held back. It was for Orson to make his own confession. He was about to tell about the shooting at the pond and on Expectro Peak, but this, too, he kept secret. If the incidents were not reported, the perpetrator of the hoax might give himself away. He had admonished Trable to keep silent and he could do no less.

The men had washed up in the creek and now crowded about the chuck wagon for chow. Sam drew Pop Keller aside and said something to him. Pop went to the front of the wagon and came back with a bottle. It was clearly a bottle of whiskey. Joel stopped Sam as he came back with the whiskey.

"What are you gonna do with that, brother? Put it in the stew?" he asked.

"No. I reckon the men deserve one slug to get the dust outta their throats," Sam replied shortly.

"Pa an' Uncle Giles made a rule—"

"To hell with the rule! Earl can keep the rule if he chooses. I aim to make my own rules," Sam cut him off.

CHAPTER EIGHT

The following day was one of hard work and excitement. The men were up at daybreak and out working the herd by sunup. The men worked in two teams. One tended to the branding. The other team tended to the castrating of the bull calves. Joel, with confidence in his horse, Volcan, elected to do the heel-roping.

Trable was roping at the head. Pete Dana, at Giles's orders, was cutting out the cattle to be branded. Giles was presiding at the other fire where Sontag was helping with the cutting job. The branding area became a noisy bedlam with the shouts of the men and the bawling of the cattle. The smell of cow dung and horse sweat permeated the pall of dust that hung over the area, dust thick enough to dim the light of the blazing sun. Ordinarily the previously branded cattle would be counted and turned loose, with only the slicks and the yearling calves being branded, but this time Giles insisted on putting his Box-G on every other head.

"It's goin' to slow up the job, Joel," Sam said during the noon break. "I don't know what's the matter with Earl. Sure all the cattle are branded BB 'cause that was the name of the ranch when it was a partnership. I don't see no reason why the herd can't be run under the BB brand with the profits divided when the cattle are sold, just like before."

"I reckon Uncle Earl wants to do his own marketin', his own bargainin', an' have nothin' more to do with us," Joel surmised.

Sam shrugged. "He's a changed man since Jim Costly was killed an' Pa put in prison."

"I reckon it started before that, Sam," Joel opined. "Giles was beginning to squirm under Pa's thumb. That's why he built his separate home ranch years ago."

"Orson marryin' a squaw didn't help matters," Sam said. "I reckon Uncle Earl still feels guilty for havin' kicked Orson out. I wonder where Orson an' his squaw are now. Out on some reservation far north, like the Jicarilla, for instance," Sam mused.

Joel felt a qualm at keeping Orson's visit to Vado a secret, but he still felt constrained to silence. Let Orson spring his own surprise in his own way on Giles and the rest of the family.

"I didn't know Orson very well, Sam. Fact is, he was outta my mind a long time ago. A kid still in his teens sure ain't much concerned with family quarrels, or their comings and goings."

"I knew him, Joel. He was a spunky, upstandin' young man, a little stubborn, mebbe, but so is Giles. Orson committed the unpardonable sin—he married a squaw. I reckon it weren't no sin in the eyes of God, but it was to his pa."

The noon break over, they went back to work. By nightfall the work wasn't finished. The herd was bedded down after drinking its fill at the creek. The dusk was punctuated with the bawling of calves indignant over the rough treatment they had received, and the bawling of cows looking for their stray calves. The men, pooped out from the heat, the dust, and the work, sloshed their heads in the creek and raked their hair back under their sombreros with their fingers.

Joel noticed the expectant air about them as they gathered around the chuck wagon. He knew they were waiting eagerly for their ration of hooch. He was a mite worried over Sam's loosening of the ban on liquor in camp. One slug of hooch was merely a prod to a drinking man, a prod that whetted his appetite and did little for his morale. One slug was often worse than nothing to a man. In fact, it affronted his dignity to some degree, denying him the right to choose how much he could have.

Joel was aware of what one too many drinks can stir up. So having a lot of hooch was no answer. On a roundup, *no* hooch was the best answer. For any amount of hooch could mean trouble. With drink, even a friendly slur can become an insult, and an insult can become a matter of pride. Once a wrong word is spoken it can be retracted only with the eating of humble pie, a dish disdained by a knight of the range.

Joel had seen wanton killings over a misspoken

word. He could object to Sam's leniency, but it would only lead to dissension between them. Sam had been the one who had stayed out of jail and taken on their father's problems. He, Joel, could do no more than keep an eye on things and try to avert trouble. He had to admit that the slug of hooch at least injected a spirit of camaraderie among the men.

After their meal of pungent stew, tangy dried fruit, sourdough biscuits, and steaming coffee, they piled mesquite roots on the waning branding fire and sat about, crosslegged, smoking afterchow quirlies and exchanging yarns. Josiah, finished with his chores, came over with his banjo to join the group.

"Is I or ain't I welcome to join you? I figgered some music might keep them abused cows quiet," he said.

"Sit down, Shuffle," Joel said, making room. "Give us a chorus of good singin'."

Shuffle plunked the banjo and raised his mellow voice in song. He went from one drinking song to another, and then switched to "Genevieve" and "Jeanie with the Light Brown Hair." Some of the men joined in the singing, and the campfire became a melodious chorus of plaintive voices in the vast stillness of the night.

In the morning the men downed their hotcakes, side meat, and coffee while the sun was still just a dim promise, and then went to work on the remainder of the cattle brought in the day before. They finished the job in the middle of the afternoon, too late to move camp to the next location, but still early enough for the men, with unexpended energy, to engage in a little horseplay. They vied with each other, making bets on who could rope and tie a calf the fastest. They cut some of the half-grown calves out of the herd for their fun. The calves were weaned so their mothers were indifferent toward them. Giles's men drifted over to join in the sport.

"I reckon the Box-G can beat anybody on the BB," Dusty Kiler opined. He was no longer young.

"Wait a minute, Dad, ain't you a mite old fer sich competition?" Herb Sontag gibed.

"Put your money where your mouth is, Sontag," Dusty said quietly.

"I'll bet a dollar," Sontag offered.

"Ain't that a mite stingy, pardner?" Dusty sneered.

"I don't want to rob you, old man," Sontag retorted.

"If you're aimin' to rob me, I'll make it worth your while. I'll put up my monthly paycheck," Dusty dared him.

It was Sontag's turn to hedge. "Ain't you bein' downright foolish, old man?" Sontag inquired.

"I ain't an *old man*," Dusty said. "If you got the guts, you can make me prove it."

Sontag fidgeted. "Choose somebody to represent you, Dusty. That way I won't feel guilty takin' your money."

"But I'd feel guilty takin' yours, Sontag. I'll make the first try. That way you can ease your conscience."

Joel stepped into the discussion. "There ain't gonna be no bets like that made. You can bet a dollar, but that's the limit. Any more than that an' this roundup'll turn into a crap game." He was thinking of Sam, bending the rule on drinking.

"What the hell do you care what we do with our money?" Dusty demanded.

"I care plenty," Joel said.

"You ain't really the rawhide behind this roundup, Badly. I reckon Sam is a mite more considerate," Hebe Rasco horned in.

"Why, Rasco? Is it because he passed the bottle around before chuck?"

"That's more'n Giles does."

"I ain't backin' Sam on his whiskey policy, Rasco. Bruce Badly, my pa, made the no-drinkin' rule an' he stuck by it. It kept trouble confined to an occasional night in town," Joel said.

"We was all one crew then," Rasco said. "Now we're two camps, an' one of the crews is gettin' favors. Either Sam is tryin' to gain the affection of his crew or he's hopin' to stir up trouble among Giles's men. In fact, we're grumblin' already, but Giles ain't about to follow Sam's example."

"Pete Dana ain't grumblin'," Oral Fibbs opined, scratching his lean and whiskered jaw.

"What do you mean by that, Oral?" Joel inquired.

"I reckon Dana's got him a bottle of hooch stashed out somewhere. Him an' his pals seem right down overcheerful at times. The fact that Giles hired Dana because he's tough and handy with a gun keeps him from enforcing the no-liquor rule on him. When Dana an' his two sidekicks traipse off by theirselves, I reckon they get a good swig or two."

Sam came over, his bushy, black hair curling from under his hat. His lean face was sober. "What's the argument here, Joel?"

Joel explained what had been going on. Sam turned on Dusty and the other Box-G riders.

"Did Giles send you men over here?" he asked.

"Nope," Dusty Kiler said, his lean, gray face defiant. "We just come over for a mite of fun."

"When a man's willin' to bet away a month's pay earned with sweat, dust, questionable chow, an' achin' bones from sleeping on the ground, there ain't no fun involved. Is Earl tryin' to stir up trouble between our two crews?"

"It ain't Earl Giles who's stirrin' up trouble, it's you with your floutin' of the rules your pa laid down. You're dolin' out likker to your men like a sugar lump to a dog what fetched your boots. Giles ain't wheedlin' us like ninnies, he's stickin' to the rule."

"I ain't my pa," Sam said, "an' I don't give a hoot what your boss does. I'll run my crew the way I see fit. You can go on with your play, but there ain't no man of mine bettin' away a month's pay on a stupid wager. The man who loses a month's pay loses interest in his job. There's no use in sweatin' for another man's profit. I reckon you was bitin' off a mite more than you could chew, Dusty. If you're so hellfire sure of your prowess, try it out against me."

Joel protested. "Wait a minute, Sam, you're just aggravatin' the situation. If you put Dusty Kiler down in front of the men, it will only rile him more. If he puts you down, it won't mean a thing. The men'll think you slackened off to let him win. Better let the men have their fun among themselves."

Sam gave him a scowling look. "Are you takin' over, brother? Your half of the authority hereabouts is questionable."

Joel felt a thrust of anger. "It may be questionable to you, but not to me. I saw Pa in the messhall of the Yuma jail before I was released. He knowed I'd be headin' back to the BB. He left no doubt in my mind that me an' you was to handle the ranch as partners. What do you aim to do, Sam, start a feud between us like that what come between Uncle Giles and Pa?"

"We'll talk about that in private, Joel," Sam said with finality. "Go on with your sport before we start a real fuss."

Sam walked away to avoid further trouble. Kiler, still smarting over the conversation, jackknifed his lean frame into the saddle of his horse.

"Anybody got a watch?" he inquired.

"I've got my pa's watch. He give it to me when I left Yuma," Joel said.

"Somebody cut me out a calf," Dusty requested. "I ain't hedgin' my bet."

"I ain't takin' your pay, Dusty. You're a prideful old man, Kiler, but I've heard that pride goeth before a fall," Sontag said.

Pete Dana, who had stayed out of the conversation, went over to the herd and cut out a hefty calf and dragged it over, to where the men were standing, on the end of his rope. Dusty shook out his loop and pulled his hat tight on his graying hair.

"Turn it loose!" Dusty cried.

Joel had his watch in his hand. The calf headed back toward the herd. Dusty's pony, trained to instinctive action, raced toward the calf. Dusty, with a tying rope in his mouth, swung his loop over the head of the calf before it was halfway back to the herd. His pony stopped stiff-legged. Dusty was out of the saddle before the calf hit the end of the rope and hurtled to the ground. He slipped the noose of the tying rope over the calf's front feet, drew up the hind feet and bound the four feet together, after some tussling.

Joel, his eyes on the second hand of the watch, felt a jab of pity. It had taken Dusty thirty-one seconds to complete the job, a poor mark. Eighteen or twenty seconds would have been closer to the mark. Joel announced the time.

"Thank me, Dusty," Sontag jeered. "I saved you a month's pay."

Dusty cursed. He glared at Joel. "Are you sure that there turnip of your pa's is keepin' good time?" he demanded.

"This turnip is doing all right. It kept time for all the prisoners in the dugout cages at Yuma. I reckon it's you who's runnin' slow, Dusty," Joel said.

"Let's see how fast you can make it, Badly. I reckon that there prison grub an' them iron cots ain't added much to your agility," Dusty snapped.

It was a direct challenge, one not to be ignored by a prideful man. Joel felt the eyes of the men upon him, waiting expectantly for his reply. He and Margo had often roped calves when they were younger, vying with each other. Sometimes he had slacked off to let her win, but she wasn't fooled. At such times she pounded him on the back with her small fists for favoring her. He saw no harm in accepting Dusty's challenge, even though his own time for roping was around twenty seconds. He couldn't afford to favor Dusty as he had Margo. The men were too smart to be duped.

"Here, Sontag, you hold the watch," he said, handing Herb the timepiece. "Somebody cut me out a calf."

Oral Fibbs wangled a yearling steer out of the herd, a hefty animal half-grown but still full of spunk. Joel mounted Volcan, and gave the signal to turn the calf loose. Volcan leaped forward like a shot. Joel had his loop shaken out, his eyes on the calf. He was about to raise his arm and make his throw when a loop settled over his shoulders, slid down his arms, jerked tight and catapulted him from the saddle. He hit the ground stunned by the unexpected attack.

Before he realized what was happening, he was straddled by a pair of chaps, and his ankles were bound securely by a tying rope. The thing was so preposterous he lay dazed for a moment unable to realize what had happened. Then his vision cleared and he saw Pete Dana getting off him and holding both hands in the air. A slow fury burned in Joel's mind and body. He lay helpless, the loop pinioning his arms, his ankles secured by the tying rope.

A raucous peal of laughter went up from the men. There *was* a touch of macabre humor in the situation, but to Joel it wasn't funny. His first impulse was to grab a gun and face Dana, but his gun had bounced from his holster in his awkward contact with the ground, and even if he had a gun he couldn't use it trussed up as he was.

He heard Dana call out, "What was my time, Sontag?"

Sontag said, "Fourteen seconds!"

Joel was blinded by fury. "Get these danged ropes off me! I don't see any humor in the situation!"

"Now you know how the calf feels, Joel!" Rasco sang out.

"No calf ever felt what I'm goin' to do to the buzzard who sneaked up an' played this trick on me!" Joel exclaimed.

"Simmer down, pardner," Trable said as he came over and released the ropes. "It was just a prank."

"I done it, Joel. I just couldn't help myself. I figgered the afternoon needed a mite of fun," Dana drawled.

Joel got up and dusted himself off. He glared at Dana. In spite of his toothy grin, Dana was a man prepared for action. It showed in the set of his shoulders and the straddle of his feet. It dawned on Joel that Dana had taken this opportunity to goad him into a showdown, passing off the provocation as a joke. Either Joel had to accept the provocation as a challenge, or squelch his anger and pretend to join in with the levity. His gun lay on the ground a few feet away, where it had fallen.

"I'm sorry you cain't take the joke, Badly," Dana continued. "You ain't no more humiliated or injured than that there calf would've been. If you need some action to get the sting outta your hurt feelin's, I can oblige you any way you want. Go ahead, pick up your gun."

Joel had regained enough sanity to realize that gunplay in the first camp of the roundup could create nothing than more dissension than there already was. But to ignore Dana's dare altogether would lessen his prestige among the men, and the prison sentence had already marked him. He turned carefully and stooped to pick up his gun prepared to meet Dana's challenge. He had no thought of killing Dana, just nicking him perhaps, or shooting the gun out of his hand.

As his hand closed over the gun, Dana's gun roared and Joel felt the splash of earth against his boot as Dana's shot furrowed the ground at his feet. It was further humiliation, designed to belittle him before the men. Furious, Joel gripped his gun and turned to face whatever threatened. He was rudely bumped by a man who appeared from nowhere. A hand gripped his wrist and twisted his gun down. He stared into the face of his Uncle Giles.

"What the devil's going on here?" Giles demanded.

"Jest a little horseplay, Earl," Rasco answered for them.

"I don't call it horseplay when guns start popping. This is supposed to be a roundup, not a rodeo. Which one of you clowns started this stupidity?"

"I reckon I did, boss," Dana said softly. "I mistook your nephew fo' one of the calves, an' roped an' tied him. He couldn't see the humor in it. I was givin' him a chance to soothe his feelin's."

"By shooting at his feet when he wasn't looking? I didn't hire you to cause trouble on the range. I hired you to prevent it. I won't stand for this kind of horseplay. You Box-G men had better get back to our camp before you get into real trouble."

Sam came up to the group. "I was down at the creek washin' the dust off my carcass. I heard the shot. What's goin' on here?"

Joel didn't try to explain it to Sam. He let Trable do the talking.

CHAPTER NINE

The next day, with the men's feelings still ruffled from the byplay of the afternoon before, Giles had his cut of the herd driven some distance toward the west away from the BB stock. It was afternoon when the cavvy got moving out along the Rio Penasco toward the west side of the Pecos. They camped that night on a stream near the foot of the Guadalupe Mountains. It was a green spot in the vast area of sand and mesquite, watered by the runoff from the hills that created a green meadow on either side of the stream.

There was feed for the horses and enough for the cattle that would be gathered. The early fall added a tang to the air in this upland location and tinted the aspen and maple along the stream with exotic colors.

The remuda of extra horses was confined in a rope corral on the best grass. And Pop Keller with the help of Josiah Shuffle soon had the camp stove steaming with coffee, steaks—cut from a yearling killed that morning—sizzling aromatically on the top of the sheet-iron stove, and sourdough biscuits browning in the Dutch oven. The men, having doused their faces in the stream and raked their hair back under their tall hats, stood about expectantly waiting for their ration of hooch. Their wait came to an abrupt end.

Sam, striding over from the chuck wagon, announced, "No hooch tonight, men. There ain't no more."

"Are you cuttin' out the hooch because of that ruckus yesterday?" Mike Stiller, one of the new men, said in an edgy voice.

"I brought just enough hooch to give you a slug to take the crest off the first couple of days on the roundup," Sam said flatly.

"Are you sure Giles didn't scare you into cuttin' out the ration?" Jag Oby, Stiller's partner, asked in a huff.

Joel came over. "What's the beef, Sam?" he inquired.

"Sam's cuttin out the ration of hooch we was gittin'," Sontag informed him.

"He shouldn't have broken the rule in the first place," Joel told them. "If Sam says there ain't no more hooch, then there ain't no more hooch."

"I reckon Giles cowered him down," Sontag grumbled, fingering the scar on his lean jaw.

"All right, why don't one of you go over an' search the supply wagon. That'll put an end to it," Joel suggested.

As Sontag headed for the supply wagon, Sam shoved Joel roughly out of earshot of the others. "Why did you tell him to search the wagon? Do you want to make me out a liar? We're supposed to be workin' together, not agin' one another."

"Stifle down, Sam." Joel grinned. "I expected something like this. I took the remainin' bottle of hooch outta the wagon an' cached it in the bedroll of Shuttle. The men won't tinker with the kid's stuff. They figger he's not likely to be hoardin' any supply of hooch."

"This roundup is already hoardin' a big supply of trouble," Sam growled. "I reckon Giles don't aim to be cooperative, and I'm still not sure all the stock gathered is reachin' the brandin' fire."

"You mean Giles is holdin' out?"

"Either Uncle Giles or else somebody else is moonlightin' with his blessin'. I reckon two can play at the same game."

"How do you mean, Sam?"

"We can overlook a few cattle here an' there in gullies or barrancas where they won't be likely to be found an' come back for 'em later."

"Won't that be cheatin', Sam?"

"It depends on how you look at it. If it comes to a showdown, I'll make Giles swear he ain't been skimmin' off a few head an' hidin' them in The Thicket or some of the broken country hereabouts."

"I don't like it," Joel said flatly.

"Look here, brother, I took over the runnin' of the BB whilst you was in jail. Now you pop up and try to tell me how to do it. Actually, you ain't got the guts to fill Pa's shoes."

"Maybe I don't want to fill Pa's shoes. His shoes was smirched with more than a little blood. He cheated when he could, rustled stock when he could get away with it, an' duped the ignorant heirs of the land grant owners outta their property for peanuts. Sure he got deeds to the land, most of 'em signed with an X."

"Are you belittlin' your own pa, Joel? He didn't do nothin' the other big ranch owners didn't do to build their herds, includin' Chisum an' Richard King. Rustlin' mavericks ain't stealin', an' them Mexican heirs to the Spanish Land Grants, never made a nickel off that wilderness an' never would have. An' as for blood on his boots, there ain't no worthwhile leader in the West that hasn't been blooded. Now your pa's in jail for a shootin' that you're as much to blame for as he is."

"I agree with all that, but things are changin' in the West. The fact that me an' Pa got convicted by a jury an' sentenced by a judge proves that, even if we didn't willfully mean to kill Jim Costly. I liked Jim. His death rides heavy on my conscience."

"Our pa didn't like him. There was something between 'em I never could figger out. Pa tolerated him because of Ma. Costly was an' upright man who treated us kids real fair, especially you an' Margo, when we was growin' up. Ma liked him for that an' his droll humor. He could make her laugh even when she was frettin' an' fussin' over the ills a ranch woman is heir to. I never could figure why Costly didn't get married. He liked kids. He could have had a batch of his own."

"People knew of the breach between Pa an' Jim. That was one of the points against us at the trial," Joel mused.

Sontag came back from the supply wagon empty-handed. Joel and Sam rejoined the group.

"Did you find anything?" Joel asked.

Sontag was flour up to his elbows from digging in the flour barrel. "I reckon Sam was tellin' the truth," he said ruefully.

Sam said, "When we get near that new camp at Carlsbad, you can swill yourself unconscious. I reckon they got three-four saloons there. May not be a church or a school, but they's bound to be saloons."

The next day they set out to round up all the cattle they could find. Joel was still riding with Trable, but Sam was about to choose Dusty Kiler, one of Giles's men, as a partner when Giles interfered.

"Look, here, Sam, I don't think it's good policy to mix our crews more than necessary. If they start quarreling out on the range, it could lead to serious trouble. Here at the brandin' fire, we can keep an eye on them."

"Who's goin' to keep an eye on 'em out on the range? Some waddies have a temptin' habit of skimmin' off a few head an' hidin' 'em for future profit," Sam said without humor.

Giles bridled. "You got anybody special in mind, Sam?"

"You've heard that old saying, Uncle Giles: 'If the shoe fits, wear it.' I ain't accusin' anybody without proper proof. We both got new tough men on our crews for obvious reasons, reasons that have no right to divide the ranch that you an' Pa built. Them men ain't got no reputations that could stand the examination of a magnifyin' glass."

"I split Dana an' his men up," Giles said. "Leiberg is riding with Fibbs, and Dobel is riding with Rasco. I'll ride with Dana myself. Does that mollify you any, Sam?"

"I reckon I got nothing to be mollified about, Earl, not yet. I aim to ride with Stiller, and Sontag will ride with Oby. Joel an' Trable get along all right together."

"Are you sure they're not getting along too good?"

"What do you mean?"

"I saw them talking together when they brought their gather in the other day. I got the impression that something happened out on the range that day, something they don't want to talk about."

"You shore don't think that Joel is rustlin' his own cattle, do you?"

"I'm just wondering. Since Joel's been home he hasn't had much to say about anything. Maybe he feels left out. Since Bruce has been in jail at Yuma, you've come to think of the BB as yours, lock, stock, an' barrel. You've left no doubt in Joel's mind that he's still a felon, disenfranchised, without the right to own property or even cast a ballot. Joel isn't like his father, thank God. He's more like his mother, but if you'll notice, your ma, Kay, usually gets her way.

"I've got a feeling that Joel doesn't feel like a felon. He's got a mandate from Bruce to share in the running of the BB on equal terms with you until Bruce gets out of jail. Try to tell Bruce that he's a felon when he gets out, and you'll learn what the wrath of God means. I'm splitting up the ranch now, while Bruce is incarcerated. I want it done before Bruce gets out of Yuma. If he was here he'd kick the guts out of my intentions as he always did. I've had my say. Let's get the crew out on the range."

Joel stopped Sam as he was leaving after his conversation with Giles. He asked what it was all about, and Sam told him, leaving out Giles's suggestion that he, Joel, might be skimming off cattle. In fact he left out all reference to the fact that Joel might be resentful of his, Sam's, high-handed ways. Joel suspected as much and as he and Trable headed out toward the hills to ferret out stock, he brought up the subject.

"I was just talkin' to Sam," Joel said.

"I know that, Joel." Trable nodded. "You look like a dog with something stuck in his craw. What's worryin' you?"

"I got a notion Sam didn't tell me half of what they talked about. I got a feelin' he's suspicious about our visit to Expectro Peak, or Giles is suspicious an' told Sam so."

"We should of spoke up in the first place, Joel," Trable opined.

"I figgered if the man who tried to kill me was one of the roundup crew, our silence might worry him into givin' hisself away."

"But you wasn't even hit, Joel. Any man with earnest murder in his heart could have killed you twice over out there in the open. It was more like he was just tryin' to scare us away; mebbe some old sourdough still hauntin' the cave."

"He put the fear of God in me. And I ain't goin' to have much peace, Archy, until I know who did get me released from prison."

All of the crews brought in sizeable bunches of cattle, and it took two days to brand, castrate, and separate them. There was a new uneasiness in the two cow camps and Joel felt it but couldn't quite understand it. For one thing, Sam was riding with Mike Stiller, the new man with the ornery temper, so Stiller couldn't do any skimming without Sam's knowledge. Giles was riding with Dana, so that let Dana out of suspicion. The rest of the gunplay crew were tagalongs, without the brains, gumption or courage to strike out on their own. So, on the surface, there didn't seem any cause for uneasiness. And a kind of guarded peace seemed to hold sway, as though everybody was satisfied with the course of events. Joel explained all this to Trable as they scoured the foothills for stock.

"Mebbe everybody is satisfied, Joel," Trable said. "The regular hands is gettin' their pay with the hope of a bonus if the count warrants it, but the gun-handy gents like Dana an' Stiller might be satisfied for other reasons. If things wasn't goin' their way, they wouldn't be so meek an' mild. Ain't there a slight possibility that Giles is turnin' his head to what Dana's doin'?"

"Oh, yeah? In your logical reasoning, that would mean Sam was coddlin' Mike Stiller. I don't buy that. Sam is pushy an' hard, almost as hard as Pa, but he ain't sneaky. He'll get what's his in the open an' face any man down for the right to it."

Trable shrugged. "A boil allus breaks when the festerin' reaches a peak. I reckon trouble is the same way. If anything rotten is goin' on, the eventual stink of it will make it known."

About the time the men were getting too grumpy to hide their feelings, and their thirst for liquor, they camped near Carlsbad. Sam was debating whether to turn the men loose for the holiday they had been promised before or after they had brought in the cattle and branded them. Joel helped with the decision.

"The men won't be worth a hoot this close to liquor an' women, Sam. They'll hurry the roundup, skippin' the cows in the chaparral an' the barrancas, and we'll have a short count. I reckon I could use a mite of relaxin' myself."

"We don't want any drunken brawls or gunfights. You an' me will have to stay reasonably sober," Sam cautioned.

Carlsbad, like most towns in the West, had grown from a campsite on the Pecos, where inquisitive people stopped on their way to visit the awesome caverns to the south, into the semblance of a town. It boasted a dusty street lined with false-front buildings housing an assay office, a saloon, a ladies' wear and dressmaking shop, a marshal's office, a second saloon, a general store, a doctor's office which also served as the mortuary, still another saloon, and Ma Frimple's boardinghouse reserved for discriminating customers.

There was also a stage station which boasted a telegraph and a two-story hotel which contained a restaurant and an additional saloon. It was a fairly busy town supported by mines, trappers, visitors eager to see the great limestone caverns, and cattlemen who ranged the Staked Plains. Heat still lingered in the fall air, and the dust was inches deep on the street, but to the cowboys who had endured the grueling labor of the roundup, it was Saint Jo and Chicago rolled into one.

The BB crew reached town with the dust beaten out of their Levi's, the clean shirts they'd carried with them for just such a holiday, and their hair raked into a semblance of order with what combs they possessed or could borrow. Their bristly faces were scrubbed clean, but with the sun and windburn one could hardly tell the difference. They bypassed the barber shop, not wishing to waste any of their short holiday sitting around waiting to be shaved.

Joel was the exception.

"You go along with the men, Sam," he told his brother. "I reckon I'll get a real shave an' haircut while I have the chance. In Yuma our hair was sawed off with a knife, an' most times we shaved with broken pieces of glass. They wouldn't allow us to have razors. Once in a while a barber came in from the town an' shaved us for the horsehair ropes or bridles we braided, or the wood carvings and stools we made outta the material from packin' cases an' put together with pegs."

Sam pushed his shaggy hair back under his tall hat. There was a worried look on his angular face. "Don't take too long with your primpin'. There could be some trouble when Uncle Giles's crew shows up. I still don't like your idea of makin' the men leave their guns in camp. I let you overrule me on that, Joel, but I ain't sure the Box-G men will be coming with no iron on their hips."

"Like I argued, Sam, unarmed men ain't provoking no gunfights. Let 'em bruise their knuckles an' get their face bashed in if they ain't got no better sense. Their bruises'll heal in a day or so. A dead man ain't goin' to be no good to us a-tall. That's why I left my gun in camp. You used your privilege as boss and brought your gun along. Let's hope it don't prove to be a mistake."

"I aim to keep the peace, not start a fight. Somebody's got to have enough clout to keep the men in line. I hear the law here ain't very heroic. I'm layin' you two to one, brother, that Dana won't come to town without his iron."

Joel pondered this. "I can't argue with that, Sam. Dana ain't just a man no more, he's a walkin' target for a dozen men that had to lick his boots. But I reckon Dana won't stir up no trouble before the roundup's over. I think he has more important plans. Just don't let the men stir up more hell than they can handle."

Joel went into the barbershop, a small dingy room with cobwebs in the corners. There was a shelf with a row of numbered mugs and a brass spittoon which showed ample evidence of having been missed as often as it had been hit. The barber chair was made of raw planks with a powder keg for a footrest.

As Joel waited for the barber to finish up with a hawk-nosed man with a dour face, he heard Giles's crew riding up the main street with whoops and yells punctured by a couple of gunshots. The gunshots worried him. Right now the men were displaying their exuberance. A couple of shots of red-eye and a smile from a painted face would soon mellow them into noisy camaraderie. The next step would be touchy pride, flamboyant bragging, and a challenge to put up or shut up. As the men passed the murky window, he couldn't tell who was doing the shooting. He felt sure it wouldn't be Dana. Men like Dana didn't waste bullets.

His face smarting from the pull of the ancient razor, and his hair clipped up to above his ears, Joel left the barbershop and went out onto the busy street. The sun was just setting, casting a weirdly beautiful design of red, violet, and orange across the evening sky. The frogs were piping down by the river, and the soft,

pungent smell of night was on the cooling air. Before
stabling his horse, Joel went into the hotel lobby to see
if he could reserve a room for the night. The rest of the
men would sleep off their drunk in the hay of the livery
barn near their horses, but he still craved the comfort
and warmth of a real bed after six months on the iron
cots at Yuma. As he entered the lobby of the hotel, he
heard someone call him.

"Oiga, senor! Buenas tardes!"

Joel swung around and stared into the cherubic face
of Porferio Diaz! "What in the name of heaven are you
doing here, Porferio?" Joel exclaimed. The boy was
dressed in new clothes with a white shirt and a string
tie. His boots were polished magnificently, and his
black Indian hair, combed neatly.

"I have come weeth the *Senorita* Layton, amigo. I
geeve her the *proteccion* and the *interpretacion.*"

"You—you mean Dorothy Layton is here, in
Carlsbad?"

"In the flesh, Mr. Badly," a soft voice said right
behind him.

He turned and looked into the radiantly defiant face
of Miss Layton's niece. He was at a loss to grasp the
situation. Then he arrived at the only logical explana-
tion.

"So, Miss Layton, you're taking my advice. Good
for you. You don't belong here in the West." Joel put
his hand on Porferio's head. "You're not serious about
taking this Mexican boy back to Boston? He'd be out
of place there, just as you are out of place here."

"Just a minute, Mr. Badly. You're getting ahead of
yourself. Who said anything about Boston?"

"Where else would you go, Miss Layton?"

"First let's dispense with the formality. I'm Dorothy and you're Joel. And I, Dorothy, am on my way to refurbish my wardrobe in a town that has proper shops, and you, Joel, have no authority to question or hinder me."

It wasn't until then that Joel became aware of her costume. His attention had been riveted on her beautiful, alive, self-confident face. Now he was puzzled and not a little amused by her clothes. She wore a divided denim skirt, one she had evidently borrowed from her Aunt Emma, and a bright flannel shirtwaist that snugly molded the alluring curves of her figure. Too snugly. And it seemed that too many buttons were left unbuttoned at the top.

"Perhaps I, Joel, ain't got no right to hinder, but I got a right to question. Where in the hell do you think you're going in that outfit you're wearin'?"

"What's wrong with my outfit?"

"Men out here ain't seen so much skin of a woman outside a saloon. If you don't button your shirt up a mite higher, you'll have a cavvy of slaverin' men followin' you around."

"Don't judge other men by the lasciviousness of your own mind, Joel Badly. A real lady can remain a lady even in her chemise."

"In Boston, mebbe, but out here I wouldn't count on it. How come your Aunt Emma let you run around alone in that getup?"

"My Aunt Emma had nothing to do with it. In fact she advised against it. She loaned me the skirt. The only blouses she had were baggy with neck-choking collars. I bought the blouse from Hilda Madson. She had some much fancier under the counter which, she said, were reserved for the *girls*."

"It ain't exactly the blouse that's invitin'. It's what's in it."

"I'm in it," she said tartly.

"Forget it. Just where are you going in that getup?"

"I'm going to Santa Fe. Porferio here says you're his *patron*. He said if he let me go alone that you would bring the *maldicion* of Saint Juan down on his head. He is my interpreter, speaking English, Spanish, and some Indian."

"I am also the wan to geeve her the *proteccion*," Porferio said.

Joel could hardly suppress a smile. "You two are a likely pair. If you're going to Santa Fe, you're off the track."

"I breeng her this way, *senor*. She want to see the roundup. She like for watch the *vaqueros* at work," Porferio volunteered.

"That was a stupid idea. The men are here in town tonight. There'll be a lot of hell-raisin' goin' on."

"Let's not stand here and argue," Dorothy said. "I'm hungry. Have dinner with me, Joel. I'm sure you can protect me from the reeky drunks who are invading the town."

"I reckon I'm about as reeky as they come, Dorothy," Joel confessed.

"You smell pleasant from here."

"That's the tonic the barber doused me with." Joel grinned.

They had a pleasant dinner and because the dining room was noisy and crowded they talked little. People raised their eyes at the sight of Porferio with the slicked-up cowboy and the beautiful girl in the strange outfit.

After dinner Dorothy said, "It's such a beautiful night, Joel, let's take a walk down by the river. I'll let you go in time to get as drunk as the rest of your men."

Joel was loath to accept the invitation, not because he was interested in getting drunk, but because somehow Dorothy Layton upset him. Oh, she interested him, all right. But at the same time he feared she just wasn't for him. It would be futile to think of a future with her. Surely, such a beautiful, educated, charming girl would soon tire of the rigors and dangers of the West, and return to the sanctuary of civilization.

The stars were bright, diamonds in a velvet sky, and the air which had cooled was like nectar, scented with the smells of sage and mesquite. The damp odor of wet, moldy leaves became stronger as they neared the water. The croak of the frogs blended with the raucous calls of the night birds like a primeval orchestra. They found a spot thick with fallen leaves, and sat down side by side. For a moment they were silent, listening to the lap and gurgle of the river.

Joel broke the silence. "I still don't know how you expect to reach Santa Fe from here, Dorothy," he said.

She put a white hand on his arm, her fingers gently pressing. "Don't—don't spoil this—this wonderful moment, Joel," she whispered.

He was puzzled by the depth of her feeling and instinctively put his hand over hers. He had the impression she was sobbing, and the feeling aroused his own emotions.

"What's—what's the matter, Dorothy?" he asked softly.

She stifled her sobs. "I don't want to burden you

with it. You wouldn't understand. You're here in the West, safe and secure in your primitive surroundings. You think that I am repulsed by the crude homes and furnishings, and the ungrammatical vernacular of the people, but for me it's an escape into an honest world free of subterfuge and vicious hypocrisy. In Boston, men and women, too, kill each other in devious ways for which there is no legal punishment. They do it by cheating, by lying, by selfishness. They commit their venial sins behind closed doors, but they can be just as murderous as any gun-toting killer. Wives *can* die of a broken heart. Men *can* destroy themselves when they are stripped of self-respect and pride and integrity."

Joel was dismayed by her castigation of the society he had always considered superior and moral.

He tried to put his feelings into words. "Stop for a minute, Dorothy. Ain't you bein' carried away a mite? If you have a confession to make, keep it for a padre. I'm a little befuddled by your confidence. We're still strangers."

"No, Joel, I don't feel strange with you. I was attracted to you the first time I saw you in Vado, and by what my aunt told me about you, and how she helped you grow up. Everything she said about you only increased my feeling. Here, seated on a couch of dry leaves and in these primitive surroundings, I felt I had to speak to you honestly. I feel I have to tell you the truth."

Joel's confusion was increased by her intimacy. She was like a child burying its head in its mother's lap, hoping for forgiveness for a wrong she was about to admit. He felt the pressure of her hand on his arm, and the warmth of it surprised him.

"If it will ease you, Dorothy, I'll listen to whatever evil sin you aim to admit," he said awkwardly.

She was silent a moment as though gathering her courage. Then she said in a shaky voice, "I was the victim of sin, Joel, not the perpetrator. I was engaged to be married to one of the eligible young men of Boston. He had gone to Harvard, and I was the envy of the other girls. To make it short, Emory Carter embezzled half a million dollars from his uncle's bank, in which he worked, to pay off his gambling debts. And, according to rumor, there was also another woman involved. When the theft was discovered, he blew his brains out."

Joel was shocked by her emotional confession. He felt the trembling of her body, and he put a protective arm about her shoulders, drawing her close to him. He felt the soft warmth of her pressed against him, and it stirred his emotions. Suddenly she was Margo in his arms. Then she was Dorothy again, with her own special charms. He saw the white oval of her face looking up from his embrace. By that compelling alchemy of nature, their lips met and he tasted the salt of her tears seasoning the warm kiss. As he released her, he heard the sound of gunshots back in the town!

CHAPTER TEN

Arriving in Santa Fe after the three days of grueling stage travel, Margo and her mother left the stage depot and walked up the street lined with adobe shops and houses, some of which were constructed before the pilgrims landed at Plymouth Rock. The Mission of San Miguel and the Governor's Palace dominated the town. The air on the seven-thousand-foot plateau, between the Pecos and the Rio Grande Rivers, was spicy with the scent of pine and cedar and the sweeter smell of roses and carnations. Clumps of lilacs, shedding their foliage with the approaching winter, huddled about some of the buildings as though snuggling together for mutual warmth.

There were more-modern buildings, some two stories high, and Elsa led the way to the most prominent on which hung a sign which read: HOTEL KEARNY. It was named after the general who had claimed the town for the United States. For one used to the primitive accommodations at Vado, the Hotel Kearny was quite elegant. Along with some of the other stage passengers, Elsa registered for one of their choice rooms.

"Ask the clerk if there's someplace that we can take a bath," Margo told her mother.

The clerk, a short, skinny man with garters on his sleeves, overheard the request. "Rest assured, madam, there's running water in your room, and a stove on which to heat it. The tub is stored upright in your closet. I'll have Selena fix your bath for you." The clerk turned his attention to the Mexican boy dozing near a corner window. The boy had on a uniform of sorts evidently taken from a soldier at the fort who had no further use for it.

"Manuel, wake up!" the clerk yelled. "Take the ladies' luggage up to their room. It's number 213."

"That sounds like bad luck already," Margo murmured.

"Don't go superstitious on me, honey," Elsa warned.

But she didn't hear her mother. Margo had her own thoughts to contend with. The strange, sublime feeling her last kiss with Joel had engendered still haunted her. Well, she mustn't think about Joel. She must try to forget him. Only, why was that so hard? She *would* forget him. She would! She'd start a whole new life. Yet why did she have to start it in Sante Fe? Deep in her heart she loved the ranching life more than anything else—and she always would. She wasn't interested in meeting young bankers or lawyers or doctors or "civilized" men.

Margo sighed deeply as she and her mother followed the boy with their bags upstairs and to the front of the hallway. He opened a door and deposited their luggage just inside the entranceway. Then he retreated to his interrupted siesta. Margo followed her mother inside and looked around. There was a rug covering most of the floor. It was a beautiful rug woven by the Navajos, with an Indian swastika design in vivid colors. The bed which she must share with her mother was wide enough and covered with a faded satin counterpane which was splotched at random with stains of spilled alcohol and whatever. Elsa opened the velvet drapes which gave the room an air of elegance.

"Well, it's livable," the older woman said. "We won't be here forever."

"*You* won't be here forever, Mother. How about me? You don't expect my wealthy, prospective husband to visit our ranch near Vado, do you?" Margo said with bitter sarcasm.

"Don't get peevish, darling," Elsa responded. "I'm quite sure you won't choose a man who will shackle you to his parlor—though you would make an attractive captive."

Their conversation was interrupted by a knock on the door. Margo opened it and faced a slim Indian girl with a calm, intelligent face and dark eyes that didn't waver.

"I have come to prepare your bath, Miss Giles. I have brought two buckets of hot water. Although there is running water at your commode, it would take quite long to start up the stove and heat it. Besides, it is too warm for a fire."

"Come on in," Margo said. "We're glad you were so thoughtful. If cleanliness is next to godliness, we're way behind the devil."

"I understand, Miss Giles," the girl said, entering and putting down the buckets. I have brought separate buckets for each of you. I would suggest you stand in the tub and wash yourselves. If you wish, I will bathe you myself."

"I—I don't think that will be necessary Miss—er—What's your name?" Elsa spoke up.

"My name is Bright Moon in Indian, but the nuns at the convent called me Selena. They said that was the name of the Greek moon goddess."

"We can wash ourselves, Selena," Margo assured her. "Where did you learn to speak English so fluently?"

"At the convent near the mission."

"How wonderful," Elsa said. She looked at Margo. "You can see in Selena how efficient the teaching of the nuns is."

"Miss Layton taught me proper English, Mother."

"But not the proprieties, dear. Playing poker with the cowboys and riding the range with Joel will never bring out a mature girl's potential. Let's not take up Selena's time with chitchat. Bring out the tub, Selena, and temper the water. You can bathe first, Margo."

When both women had bathed and were dressed and presentable, it was time for dinner.

"We'll have to make these wrinkled dresses do for tonight, honey," Margo's mother said. "Tomorrow we'll shop."

As they walked through the dining room in which the bracket lamps and chandeliers had already been lit,

Margo was aware of women in smart dinner gowns dining with men in white shirts and dark suits. The odor of roast beef and boiled cabbage was subdued by the hum of conversation.

The conversation died down and Margo was aware of all eyes being turned on her. The women's eyes envious and the men's eyes calculating. It embarrassed her because she did not know if they stared at her in her wrinkled dress because she was a naive country bumpkin or because she was actually attractive. Her doubt was dispelled soon after they were shown to a table. A youngish man in creased trousers and a garish ascot tie that snuggled under his receding chin came to their table before they had a chance to order anything. He bowed stiffly from the waist and flashed an ivory smile.

"Pardon the intrusion, ladies. Strangers in Santa Fe must be warned about the pitfalls in this very old town that is just now struggling for gentility."

Margo looked him straight in the eye. "Perhaps we should have been warned about you, sir," she said tartly.

The smile never faded. "I'll admit it, my intrusion was very abrupt, but I hoped to meet you before some buffoon attempts to embarrass you with his advances. My name is Phibius Hackwilder, barrister and adviser to the Governor."

Margo, miffed by the man's cheeky manner, said archly, "We have no need of a lawyer, Mr. Hackwilder. As for buffoons, we hope to choose our own once we are settled."

Elsa spoke up. "Ignore my daughter, Mr. Hackwilder. We've been on the road for three days and nights.

That's enough to make one petulant. Won't you sit down. I'm Elsa Giles, and this is my daughter, Margo."

Phibius acknowledged the introductions by grasping Elsa's hand and kissing it. Margo kept her hands in her lap. As he sat down he said, "I hope I am not embarrassing you."

"We're attracting attention, if that's what you mean," Margo said bluntly.

Elsa ignored her. "What was it you wanted to advise us on, Mr. Hackwilder?"

Hackwilder, smoothing back his dark, oily hair, launched into a lecture about the wines, advising only those imported from New Orleans. He cautioned them about the meat which was locally slaughtered and aged. He warned them about becoming involved with subtle crooks always on the lookout for rich, eligible girls to dally with. And when the waiter came to take their order, he offered to order for them. At that Margo took umbrage.

"Thank you, Mr. Hackwilder, but there will be no need of that. My mother and I are adults, preferring to select our own food, our own wine, and our own company, which exludes interlopers too brash to be civil."

Her voice carried across the room and started a buzz of conversation. Phibius stiffened, his weak chin thrust out, but his cheekiness was undaunted.

"Here in the West civility is a quality much to be applauded, and is more often found lacking even in strangers," he said stiffly.

Margo felt a slow burn reddening her cheeks. She felt his rebuke and it embarrassed her.

Elsa stepped into the breach. "We mean no offence,

Mr. Hackwilder," she said calmly, assuming a share of Margo's blunt appraisal of him, "but we're both tired and in no mood for blunt intrusions. Perhaps at another time, sir."

Margo felt the covert looks of the other diners, and was about to suggest to her mother that they retire from the stupid situation and have dinner sent to their room, when there was the swish of satin, a whiff of exotic perfume, and the sound of a friendly voice.

"Why, Elsa, darling, what in the world are you doing here? I haven't seen you since I was a bridesmaid at your wedding to Earl!"

Elsa rose, a look of amazed recognition on her face. "Why—why, Leffa, I might ask you the same thing. I thought you had moved to Washington when you married Senator Skaggs, who was out here on an inspection tour?"

"I did, Elsa."

"Is the Senator here with you?"

"No. He died some time ago. He succumbed to Washington dinner parties and John Barleycorn. I married again. I'm Mrs. Leffa Demargo now."

"Demargo? You—you mean the Governor of the territory?"

Leffa turned to Hackwilder, who was taking it all in. "Go peddle your papers someplace else, Hacky. These women have no use for you. They're under my protection."

When Phibius had gone, Leffa said, "We can't stand here gossiping, Elsa. You're not staying in this fleabag of a hotel. There's plenty of room up at the Palace. Henry will have your bags brought up. But first, we're dining here with some friends. I insist that you join us."

Margo took in the conversation with interest and curiosity. Leffa Demargo was a vigorous, large-boned woman with black hair that was elaborately styled. She was still handsome and her white satin gown with its red pattern emphasized the tawny color of her skin and molded the contours of her figure. Margo remembered her mother used to mention Leffa now and then years back.

"We're rather tacky, Mrs. Demargo—or should I call you *your grace*?" Margo said without waiting to be introduced.

"This is my daughter, Margo," Elsa made haste to explain.

"My, what a beautiful girl," Leffa exclaimed. "Are your other children just as pretty?"

"I have no other children," Elsa said, tight-lipped. "That's something we can discuss in private, Leffa."

As they approached the table on Leffa's heels, the men stood up. The Governor was a portly man with thinning hair turning gray. His round, florid face radiated congeniality. When they were introduced, he took Margo's hand in both of his and held it possessively.

"You're a beautiful woman, Miss Margo," he said, his eyes devouring her. "I hope your stay with us will be a long one."

"She'll be nearby," Elsa explained, "but she'll be living at the convent. I brought her to Santa Fe to be educated and polished."

When they were seated, Leffa said, "I'd like you to meet Paul Jones here." She indicated the guest and his thin, haughty wife. "He's the territorial delegate to Congress. He can't vote on legislation, but he flourishes on fringe benefits and bribes he gets for doing favors. He's no relation to John Paul Jones."

"You're nasty, Leffa," Mrs. Jones said in a squeaky voice. "There's no such thing as a bribe. They're legal fees."

The Governor changed the subject. "That convent is a dreary place, my dear," he said to Margo. "There's mostly Indians, Mexicans, and a few Cajuns who drifted over from Louisiana. But the nuns are good teachers, I'll grant them that."

They talked as they ate, mostly about things Margo was ignorant of. She learned that the former governor of the territory had been shot in a duel, and Demargo had been appointed by President Hayes because of his help during the election. Margo sipped the wine sparingly, but Elsa seemed to relish it. When weariness threatened to overcome her, Margo suggested that she be excused to go up to the room.

"No, honey," Leffa objected, "you might be chewed up by bedbugs. I'll take you and your mother up to the Governor's Palace, and the men can stay here and do whatever it is men do when their wives are away. Our carriage is just outside."

"I'll go with you," Mrs. Jones said. "You can drop me off at my house."

The room at the palace was larger than the hotel room and was decorated in much better taste. It had an oriental rug on the floor, and the velour drapes showed no signs of age. There were two beds.

"I'm giving you this room so you can sleep together. It's rather haunting in this place, with its ghosts of two hundred years. You will be company for each other."

"If you don't mind, I'll lie down," Margo said. "If you want to talk over your younger days, go ahead. I'll probably fall asleep."

"I'll get you a nightgown," Leffa offered.

"Thank you, Mrs. Demargo. I'd appreciate that."

Moments later, while Margo got ready for bed, the two older women had their heads together near the crystal-shaded lamp on the center table. Margo slid between the crisp, white sheets, but she didn't sleep at once. She was intrigued by the low conversation between the two women near the table.

They laughed over old escapades, some of which were rather scandalous. They talked of old loves, and it sounded as if they'd had as many friends among the barroom girls in those days as they'd had among the respectable gentry. Margo finally drifted off into a deep sleep of exhaustion. When she awoke, the sun was bright and she found her mother dressed and seated by a commode while a beautiful Spanish girl was arranging her mass of dark hair.

"Good morning, sleepyhead. I've already had my bath, and the houseboy has refilled the tub for you."

"Good morning, Mother," Margo said, eager for the bath. "Has the houseboy gone?"

"The houseboy is gone. Our maid, here, is Isabella," Elsa said. "You can bathe in the alcove. There's a curtain to give some privacy."

Isabella, a tall, shapely girl with flashing eyes and black hair braided about her head like a crown, offered to bathe Margo after she finished with Elsa's hair, but Margo refused the offer. She scampered to the alcove, pulled the curtain closed, and languished in the lukewarm water.

Refreshed by the bath, she donned her wrinkled dress and combed her blonde hair. Then she went down for the buffet breakfast, served off the mantel in the dining room. The Governor's Palace was a stately building for this isolated country. The ceilings were high, the rooms large. The walls had been repainted many times and the original red tiles of the floor, that had been made by the Indians under the guidance of the padres, had been replaced with decorative tiles from Spain. The Governor proved to be a genial host and Leffa extended herself for her girlhood friend.

"I'll go shopping with you, Elsa, to see that the shopkeepers don't cheat you. You can charge what you buy to my account and settle up with me later," Leffa told her.

"I think I had better take Margo to the mission and talk to the nuns before we buy too much. They might have rules for the clothing," Elsa suggested.

"You make me feel like a runny-nosed kid starting in kindergarten," Margo interposed. "Perhaps all I'll need in the convent is a wimple, a gown, and a string of beads. Did Mother explain why she rushed me off here to a convent?" Margo said to Leffa.

"She told me last night after you were asleep. It's not so odd for cousins to fall in love. It's what they do about it that's important," Leffa consoled her.

Yes, Margo said to herself, it's what they do about it. She said aloud, "I imagine that by now Joel has forgotten me. By the time the roundup's over he'll probably console himself with Miss Layton's niece who got off the stage in Vado. She was a beauty from Boston. Or maybe he'll choose Lou Parker who works in the Vado Queen."

"Don't be bitter, honey," Elsa said. "When you get settled here and meet people of importance and refinement, you'll forget all about Vado and Joel Badly."

Margo didn't argue the question. If she must settle for another man, he would just be a substitute for Joel. At least that's how things seemed to her right then. She followed her mother down the street crowded with a mixture of brown, red, and white faces.

The mission was apart from the town, gleaming brightly in its new coat of whitewash. The whitewash covered the scars of two centuries of wind, storm, and attacks by unfriendly Indians. The Convent of San Miguel was connected to the mission by a long row of shops and living quarters. As Margo entered the cool interior, she felt as though she were shutting out the real world to be held captive here with the other nuns and novices. In the cool interior of the chancellery her fears were mitigated by the kindly Mother Superior. Elsa explained why they were there, and there was some discussion about Margo's not being accepted because of her age.

"Most of our pupils are much younger. When a girl is old enough or strong enough to do any sort of menial work, the family takes them out of school to weave blankets or rugs, grind corn with a stone pestle, or herd the small flocks of sheep. We do have some older Spanish girls learning the art of proper conduct, but they help us with the younger children."

"I'm sure I could do that," Margo said. "I haven't had much chance to enjoy children, but I'm sure I would love them."

Elsa was dubious about the arrangement. "Within

two or three years you should be married, Margo. You might become too attached to the convent, and become satisfied with the children here instead of having children of your own."

"I'm sure we could guard against that, Mrs. Giles," said the Mother Superior, a buxom woman of fifty with her black robe and white halo of a wimple. "She doesn't impress me as one yearning to be a bride of Christ. There's too much restlessness in her."

"We'll talk it over," Elsa said.

"What's there to talk over, Mother? You brought me all the way up here to study at the convent. What did you expect it to be like? At least I'll feel safe here."

"Perhaps too safe, honey. It won't hurt to think it over for a day or so," Elsa said tartly.

Later, back in their room at the Governor's Palace, when they were talking to Leffa, Elsa expressed her doubts. "I'm not sure the convent is the right place for Margo," she told Leffa. "In that restricted environment, and with the children to amuse her, she might get strange ideas."

"Will you quit discussing me, Mother, as though I were a nincompoop. You're dismissing the convent because you think I'll be shut away from eligible men, and you have your heart set on seeing me marry someone important. I'll marry whom I please and when I please, and it won't be a pot-bellied banker or politician, nor one of their silly and immoral sons. I'll be no field for the sowing of their wild oats."

"That's a rather drastic indictment, Margo," Leffa chided her. "All men aren't lechers because they're rich or important. At any rate, there's an exclusive school here in town run by a well-educated and polished woman for the benefit of the daughters of the better-off families. There would be sufficient contact there with the right sort of young men. Her girls all marry well. I'm sure that with your beauty and spunk you would have no trouble in attracting a man you could tolerate if not actually become romantically involved with. The Countess Foch is discreet."

"It sounds like a slave market. 'What am I bid for this young filly, sound of wind and limb? A beauty to grace any parlor and stir envy in the hearts of men less fortunate than her owner!'"

"Stop it, Margo!" Elsa chastised her. "You're being downright impudent. After you live here a while, your values could change."

Margo ended the argument. She conceded that perhaps, after all, the finishing school would be the best place for her. She might contrive a match that would please even Elsa. She wanted time to think.

Later, when the women had gone, Isabella came in with a pitcher of water for the basin on the commode.

"How did you like the convent, *senorita*?" she inquired.

"I don't know. I'll have to think it out," Margo replied.

"Don't go there, amiga. You will be looked down on and your prospects for marriage will be little above a peon."

"Better to love a peon, than sell your soul to the devil," Margo said.

"Your love for the peon would fade after the third child, but the hard work would go on forever. At the Countess Foch's school you might dazzle a rich man and live in luxury. To hell with love. One girl came from a very strict family. Her parents made her miserable. Then she married a rich man. And now she can do anything she wants."

Margo felt a surge of rebellion. Why not? She couldn't have Joel. "I must do what Mother wants," she said flatly. "She's paying my bills." But the thought of marrying a rich man bemused her.

CHAPTER ELEVEN

With Dorothy Layton's kiss still warm on his lips, Joel was jerked back into reality by the sound of the gunshots reverberating from the town. He jackknifed to his long legs and helped Dorothy to her feet. The sound of the gunshots, two of them blending into one, was portentous. It was too early in the evening for drunken horseplay. Dorothy brushed off the dried leaves from her clothes, then clutched his arm.

"What's the matter, Joel? What is it?" she asked softly.

"It sounds like trouble, Dorothy. I've got to get back to town. If Sam's in a jam, I've got to help him," he said. "I'll drop you off at the hotel."

"Aren't you being hasty?" Dorothy asked. "Cowboys are always shooting off guns."

His hand was a little rough as he rushed her up the bank of the river. "I reckon them shots wasn't playful," he said grimly.

"Why do you say that," Dorothy inquired, panting to keep up with him.

"Because of the sequence. Them two shots blended, but they was from different guns."

They were running when they reached the top of the bank. "You go on, Joel, I'll make my way to the hotel."

Reluctantly Joel ran ahead of her. He saw men milling about under the murky light in front of the Eagle Bar blocking the bar doors. The sight confirmed his conviction that trouble had erupted. The breech between the Box-G men and the BB riders had widened in the past few days, and a bottle of red-eye could ignite touchy tempers.

"What the hell's goin' on here?" he panted, elbowing his way through the cursing, jabbering men.

"It was a fair fight!" Tom Crawley of the BB exclaimed.

"I reckon you're a liar, Crawley!" Dusty Kiler of the Box-G accused.

Expecting no coherent information from the heated threats and accusations of the men, Joel forced his way inside the bar. In the halo of light under one of the hanging lamps, Sam Badly stood, his legs braced and his gun still in his hand. In front of Sam lay the body of a man flat on his back, with his outstretched arms prepared to embrace heaven or hell, whichever came first.

A cadaverous man with a tobacco-stained beard was kneeling over the fallen man, swabbing a wound in his chest. Another man with a marshal's badge on his open vest was standing next to Sam. The tableau shocked Joel into immobility for a moment. He heard the marshal say, "How is he, Doc? Is—is he dead?"

"Not yet. Give me a hand, some of you men. We've got to get him to my office," the doctor said. "I can't do more for him here."

As Joel came out of his shock, the marshal snapped a handcuff on Sam's limp left wrist.

"What's goin' on here, Sam?" Joel managed to gasp.

Sam was in shock himself. Before he could answer, the marshal spoke up. "Ain't no time to talk to him here, mister. You a friend of his'n?"

"Brother," Joel said, still unable to believe what he saw.

"You can talk with the prisoner over at the jail if you're his kinfolk," the marshal said. He was a big, heavy man, radiating authority. There was a set to his jaw that brooked no argument. Joel was disturbed to see Sam meekly surrender his gun to the marshal and follow him out of the bar.

Joel, getting his emotions under control, followed them while the crowd of men parted to let them through.

One man said loudly, "Them's Bruce Badly's boys. Bruce cut a wide swath from here to the Mimbres, ridin' tall in the saddle. Now he's in the fed prison in Yuma. Joel bribed his way out of a three-year sentence. His pa's still in there fer five years, more or less. Now I reckon Sam will go to meet his pa, if he ain't hung for murder."

Joel clenched his fists as he heard the words. His

instinct was to fight back, but reason cautioned that one fight was enough for the night. He heard Arch Trable speak on behalf of the BB.

"Better shut your big mouth, hombre, before somebody shuts it for you!" Trable warned.

Joel didn't hear any more. His mind was concentrated on Sam and what had happened to force him into a shootout and then caused him to surrender meekly to the law.

At the jail, the jailer let his booted feet down off the desk and went to stir up the fire under the coffee pot.

"What you got this time, Klinger?" the jailer asked the marshal.

"I ain't rightly sure. I'm puttin' him in jail for his own protection," the marshal said.

Joel was allowed to go into Sam's cell with him.

"I'll be out in my office with a shotgun handy," the marshal said. "I ain't sure what brought all this ruckus to a head, but there's some hotheads out there might try to dispute my authority."

Joel sat on the iron cot beside Sam. "Now what the hell's this all about, Sam? How come you gave in so meekly to the marshal?"

"To stop a general shootout, buddy. I don't understand the thing myself."

"What do you mean? What's so mysterious about it? Who was the hombre you drawed on?"

"I don't know him. He come into the bar, guns cleared for action. He picked me out. He called me all kinds of names to get me riled. Then he yelled, 'You Badlys has been struttin', stealin' an' killin' your way to top saddle long enough! I reckon if the prison cain't hold you, a bullet can!' I told him he was maligning my father. He yelled that the sons had to pay for their father's sins. 'I'm squarin' things for Jim Costly!' he declared."

"Are you sure you ain't got no notion who the hombre was? Didn't you ask his name?" Joel inquired.

"I didn't get no chance. He shot at me whilst the men at the bar dived for cover. His bullet nicked my arm. The next thing I knew, my gun was clear of leather and firing a shot at him. I didn't aim to kill him, but he was drunk an' weavin' back an' forth."

"Mebbe he ain't dead?" Joel hazarded.

"I don't know," Sam said dully.

Then a thought flashed into Joel's mind. "He didn't call you by your first name, did he?"

"No, just Badly. Why?"

"I still ain't convinced but that Ma was right. The man might have mistook you for me. As Ma said, somebody had me sprung from jail so they could execute me. He mistook you for me, Sam!"

"I don't know, Joel. Jim Costly was workin' for Uncle Giles before you an' me was born. I ain't never seen that man with Jim, or even near the Box-G."

"That's just it, Sam. The man you shot ain't the real man who wants to square things for Costly. He was hired by the man who had me released."

Sam let this sink in. "That's a damfool setup. The man had to be a stranger if he couldn't tell me from you. I'm dark an' shaggy. You're light an slick. This business puts us in a hell of a hole. We can't delay the roundup. Every day we lose costs a lot of money. Besides, winter ain't far off. I reckon the marshal ain't gonna turn me loose until this thing is settled."

"It was pure self-defense, wasn't it?"

"That don't let me off without a court hearin'. Kangaroo courts ain't popular in the West no more. These new brand of marshals is bendin' over backward to make everything look legal. You saw how it was in Roswell at your an' Pa's trial. You was convicted on the evidence of peons who couldn't even understand what was goin' on."

Joel shook his head. "Well, they saw what they saw. Pa fired the gun an' I pushed Costly into the path of the bullet. It was a gruesome misunderstanding. Pa meant to scare Jim, an' I meant to save him, but the peons told only what they saw."

"That's water under the bridge, brother. You take charge of the roundup. Keep an eye on Giles an' his men. I still have a suspicion they're skimmin' off some of the cattle. Don't call him on that until you get clear evidence, then stand up to him."

The marshal appeared outside the cell. "I reckon I'll have to ask you to leave, mister," he said to Joel. "I understand you're Bruce Badly's boys. I knew Bruce years ago when we were young. He was pushy and brash, but that's the way the West was then. I'm Marshal Klinger, sent out here because the former marshal wasn't doin' his job. I gotta hold you until we know whether your victim dies or lives. Then we'll hold a hearin'. The circuit judge won't be here for some time. There ain't nothin' I can do until he gets here."

Joel left the jail, angry and befuddled. This was a complication he had not foreseen. He had warned Sam about bringing his gun to town, but this shootout couldn't be blamed on Sam. Sam had shot his attacker only after the man had got off the first shot. He was still disturbed by a feeling of guilt. He felt sure the man had mistaken Sam for him. The man had faced the first Badly he had come to. He knew that until he had found the person who had had him released from prison, he could never rest easy. Now he was the sole ramrod on the BB end of the roundup. He headed back to the Eagle Bar and found the men still discussing the shooting but in subdued tones. When he entered the bar, they turned to look at him.

"What the hell's it all about, Joel?" Tom Crawley asked, shoving his tall hat back on his head.

"Did Sam have enemies over thisaway?" Sontag asked.

Hebe Rasco of the Box-G opined, "I reckon Bruce had enemies scattered about long before he shot Jim Costly. Somebody's takin' out their revenge on the Badly sons."

"They goin' to hold Sam?" Oral Fibbs asked. "It was self-defense pure an' simple."

"They ain't nothin' pure an simple anymore, boys," Joel told them solemnly. "They got the same kind of legal court-an'-jury law that sent me an' Pa to prison. The marshal claims he has no recourse but to hold Sam until they find out if the man who was shot lives or dies. Then Sam has to have a hearin' in court with witnesses to clear him of the charges. In the meantime, we go on with the roundup same as before. I'm in charge for the BB."

"If we all go back to camp, who's gonna be a witness for Sam?" Archy Trable inquired.

"I reckon I'll be a witness for him," the barkeep said, "and so will my swamper or any of these men who still happen to be around when the hearing takes place."

It was well after midnight when Joel got back to the

hotel. He had intended to talk to Dorothy and explain what had happened at the Eagle Bar, but he was sure she would be asleep and he had no right to disturb her. After all, she was still a stranger to him in spite of the intimate talk they had shared down on the riverbank. He was still confused about her future plans, but his own dilemma was more pressing at the moment. Was the tragic death of Jim Costly going to hound him to the grave? He had no alternative but to run or stay and fight back. He could never turn himself back into the prison at Yuma to insure his safety. That barren hell of doomed men with its caves and bars surrounded by a thousand miles of desolation would be a fate worse than death.

Because of the excitement of the night before that lasted until after midnight, Joel didn't wake up until the warm sunlight was streaming into his room. He got up and dressed, his guilty feeling for having slept in late assuaged by the knowledge that the rest of the men would be sleeping off their hangovers or having a drink of the hair of the dog that bit them. He pulled on his Levi's and boots, washed his face in the cool water on the commode, and combed back his reddish-blond hair. Remembering his intimate talk with Dorothy the night before, the prospect of having breakfast with her was exhilarating.

Her frank and emotional confession was still clear in his mind. She was a girl deeply hurt and ostracized by her friends because of her fiance's transgressions. She needed sympathy and support and the fact that she should come to a wild, untamed frontier to find the courage to go on, proved how desperate her need was. He donned his tall hat and left the room.

Once in the lobby of the hotel he inquired if Dorothy Layton had come down for breakfast or if she was still in her room.

"She is no longer here, Mr. Badly," the clerk informed him.

"No longer here? What do you mean? There's been no stage through here during the night, has there?" Joel responded.

"No, no stage. I heard her making arrangements with Captain Koenig, who pilots a newfangled paddle-wheel boat on the Pecos River, to travel north with him as far as he goes. She was the first one down for breakfast and she left with the captain two hours ago."

Joel pondered this. Dorothy was a remarkably adventurous woman. A river freight boat carried a crew of nondescript men in whose company any female would be a temptation hard to resist. True, the small vessel would accommodate no more than three crewmen, excluding the captain, and it certainly would have no conveniences such as Dorothy of Boston had been raised to expect.

"Was there a boy with her?" he inquired.

"Yes, a Mex kid who insisted he was her protector and interpreter. They were a strange pair. The woman, Miss Layton, was a beauty, but the kid looked like a caricature in his white shirt and tie. Were they friends of yours?"

Joel remembered the night before, her emotional upset and the kiss they shared before the gunshot broke things up. He wondered what might have happened had there been no gunshot. Here he was, emotionally involved with two women, neither of whom he could hope to marry.

"She was an acquaintance of mine," Joel replied to the clerk's question.

"I figured as much. She left a note for you," the clerk said, taking a folded paper out of the mail slot.

"Thanks," Joel said, taking the note. He retired to a corner of the lobby to read the note in private. Her leaving without telling him good-bye disturbed him. The note could be her farewell gesture, but he had no notion why she had boarded a riverboat on the Pecos. Farther north the river narrowed and this season of the year could accommodate nothing more than a canoe. He opened the note and read:

Dear Joel: I am leaving Carlsbad without saying good-bye in person. Not because of indifference, but just the opposite. Our embrace at the river aroused an emotion in me that I am trying to subdue. You would have tried to prevent me from taking the boat, and I might have succumbed to your arguments. Don't worry about me. I'll probably get off the boat in Roswell and take a stage from there to Santa Fe. Perhaps I'll see you back in Vado. Do you mind if I sign off *with love*? Dorothy.

The note left him with a vacant feeling. He had hoped to see her before she left, and he would have argued against her going. Perhaps her solution had been the wisest one. He folded the note and put it in his pocket. Why he didn't burn it at once he couldn't say.

The note was a tenuous thread between him and Dorothy Layton, and he was loath to break it.

He left the hotel, determined to get on with the roundup. It was his sole responsibility now. He rousted the men out of their blankets in the hay, or the back room of the Eagle. He ate breakfast at Chinese Charley's Cafe near the bar, and then started for the jail to have a last word with Sam. Outside the cafe he ran into his Uncle Earl.

"I heard all about the ruckus and killing last night, Joel," Giles said. "You Badlys are aptly named. Bad situations tag along at your heels."

"It weren't no fault of Sam's, Uncle Earl. The crazy ranny got in the first shot without asking any questions. I ain't sure he was after Sam."

"What do you mean?"

"I reckon he was after me. Somebody sprung me from the Yuma Prison, so they could execute me like they figgered I deserved. He shot the first Badly he came to."

"Did you know the man?"

Joel shook his head. "No. I figger he was hired by the man who wants me dead—some coward too scared to do his own killin'."

"Aren't you jumping to conclusions, Joel? Who put that notion in your head? Your pa had plenty of enemies, and Sam's adding to the list. That killing last night is just an addition to the list."

"It wasn't a killin', Earl," Joel corrected him. "The man was alive when they carried him over to Doc's office. Did he die durin' the night?"

"I wouldn't know. Where are you heading now?"

"I'm goin' to talk with Sam at the jail. I'm runnin' the

BB end of the roundup on my own now, and I want to hear if he's got any special suggestions."

"Tell Sam I'll be over to see him later. After all, we're more or less of the same blood. I learned considerable about the law from my father. I'll represent him at the trial if he wants me to."

Joel continued on toward the jail a little dubious about Giles's offer and Sam's acceptance of it. He found Sam seated on the edge of his bunk staring out of the barred window. Sam rose on his long legs and gripped the bars as he talked to Joel.

"Have you heard if the man I shot died?" was his first question.

"No, I got up late after the ruckus last night. I've rousted the men out with orders to go back to camp as soon as they've had breakfast. Have you been talking to the marshal since I left?"

"He ain't changed his mind," Sam said. "He was a young officer in the Reb Army durin' the war, an' the fact that we're Yankees ain't likely to mellow his mind. Do something for me, Joel."

"Name it."

"Send a telegraph to Ma at Vado, explainin' what happened. She can send her answer here to me. Maybe she can find me a lawyer."

Joel explained Earl Giles's offer of legal assistance. Sam ran a hand through his tangled black hair, and his face hardened.

"Don't you think I'd be a mite foolish to place my defense in the hands of a man who resents and mistrusts me?" Sam asked.

"I dunno. I reckon Earl might lean over backwards to make sure you get a fair trial to prevent his bein' accused of lettin' you down on account of prejudice. After all, blood's thicker than water, they tell me. Anyhow, he's comin' over to talk to you. I gotta go now. We have to get the roundup over before the winter sets in."

Back at the camp the men rounded up the scattered cattle, branded them, checked over the count, and prepared to move in a couple of days. Two days later, as the cavvy rode on to the next camp, Crawley had a few words with Joel.

"I been ridin' after stock with Sam until now, Joel. I don't know whether I should tell you this or not, but now that you're ramrod, I figger you should know. Sam's been skimmin' off cattle."

"He's what?" Joel demanded.

"We been cuttin' out a few head here an' a few head there an' drivin' 'em into the gullies an' barrancas where we can pick 'em up later. Before you start gettin' riled up, let me explain. Sam figgers Giles is skimmin' the herd an' he aims to do a little skimmin' to even things up. In certain locations there's some meager bunches of cattle bein' brought in compared to last year."

Joel pondered this. "Mebbe Giles isn't doin' the skimmin'. Maybe it's Dana and his sidekicks. They could be stashin' cattle here an' there to be collected after they're paid off at the end of the roundup. Then they could come back an' collect them cattle as a bonus."

"You aim to accuse Dana openly?"

"Let it ride for now. We don't want no more shootings until the roundup is over. We'll keep our eyes open an' check the take against last year's tally," Joel said.

CHAPTER TWELVE

The roundup went on swinging up to the Rio Hondo south of Roswell, where it veered west at the foot of the Capitan Mountains. The BB range surrounded the Mescalero Indian Reservation and ended at the San Andreas Mountains that bordered the *Jornada Del Muerto*, The Journey of Death, a valley so named because of a company of Spanish soldiers who were ambushed by the Indians and slaughtered there. From there it turned south to the Mexican border. It was a difficult range to police because of the Indians straying off the reservation and the Mexican bandits straying across the border, all in search of cattle.

With Sam in jail, the tension between the two camps on the roundup increased. Giles assumed that his position was above that of Joel and that he should have the final word in any dispute. Joel humored him up to a point, because he was still under the stigma of being a jailbird and wanted no open quarrel with his uncle while they were still on the roundup.

So the tension between the two camps increased, and Joel felt the silent rebuke of his men because he didn't take a firm stand against Giles. Firm stands usually invited opposition which could erupt into a quarrel, the outcome of which could spell disaster.

He had little time to ponder on Sam's fate in Carlsbad or Margo's progress in Santa Fe. He worried more over the fate of Dorothy Layton on her madcap journey. Perhaps her beauty and the peculiar law of the West, which respected the virtue of a *good woman*, might see her through. On one leg of the roundup, when they were camped in the foothills below the towering peak of El Capitan, Joel stopped Archy Trable, with whom he was still a partner.

"I'm takin' off here, Arch, an' followin' Giles. He's ridin' with Dobel today. I heard a rumor he's hidin' some of the pickup to be added to his herd after the roundup. You get along without me for a while."

"I might git along without you permanent, amigo. Accordin' to your story, you're still bullet-bait for the man who got you out of jail. If Giles is skimmin' off cattle an' he finds you spying on him, you could be in one hell of a fix. Don't you reckon I should traipse along with you?"

"No, Arch. Two men is twice as easy to spot as one man."

"Mebbe so, but it seems like too many people are doin' a mite of skimmin'. You aim to do the same?"

"Hell no!" Joel said firmly. "There ain't no sense or

profit in that kind of stupidity, even if Sam's been doin' it, too. At the end of the roundup I aim to lead a pickup crew to find the stashed cattle an' bring 'em in for an honest count."

Joel took off across the undulating country, keeping to the cover of chaparral, barrancas, and sand hills. On every rise he scanned the country ahead of him and at one point he saw two riders, whom he took to be Giles and Dobel, tailing a sizeable bunch of cattle up a draw. At one place they stopped and Joel, riding to another vantage point near which they would pass, saw one of the men deliberately cut out five head of cattle and chase them up a side draw out of sight. Riding in the bottom of an eight-foot-deep barranca in the same direction as the cattle that were being hidden, he came out a mile farther on and mounted a sand hill that gave him a good view of the country below. It also made him an easy target silhouetted against the sky.

As he started to focus his eyes to the distance, he felt the crushing blow of a bullet before the sound of the rifle reached him. Before he realized he was hit, there was another whine of a bullet. Volcan reared up squealing! Joel, unnerved by the shock of the bullet, fell to the ground, stunned. Then a hard object struck him in the head bringing complete unconsciousness. The sound of another shot nearby jarred him back to a hazy reality. Everything was fuzzy but the pain in his shoulder. Suddenly he heard Trable's voice, garbled at first, and then it became clear, fraught with emotion.

"I told you you shouldn't ride out alone, amigo. I tailed you in spite of your objections. If I hadn't, you could have laid here in the sun until you rotted. Where did the bullet hit you?"

"Ain't it obvious? The left side high on the

shoulder." Joel indicated the spot. "Somebody hit me in the head, Arch."

"I reckon you was kicked by one of Volcan's hoofs."

"Where's Volcan? Is—is he dead?"

"I ain't sure. When I reached you, he was squealin' an' clawin' at some man who was tryin' to grab his reins. The man took a shot at him. When he fell, his stompin' hoofs bashed in the man's head."

"My God!" Joel said contritely. "Ain't trouble never goin' to stop? Who was the man?"

"He's Bull Dobel—that is, he *was* Bull Dobel. He was supposed to be ridin' with Earl Giles, wasn't he?"

"That's what I figgered, Arch. There was two men rousting them cattle down yonder, but I couldn't make out who they was. I don't want to accuse Uncle Earl without more proof."

"How you goin' to explain Dobel's bashed-in head?" Trable reminded him.

"It won't be too hard. We'll say we found him kicked in the head by his horse. We don't have to explain how it happened," Joel suggested.

"I'd better look at your shoulder, amigo," Trable said, unbuttoning Joel's flannel shirt. He untied the bandana from around Joel's neck and wiped away the blood. The examination didn't take long. "You was lucky, Joel. The slug went in on an angle an' glanced off the bone, comin' out the back. I'll bind it with your bandana. That'll stop the bleeding."

Joel looked at Volcan, lying motionless on the ground. Volcan was the only killer in the incident, and now he was dead. The thought sickened him. Then, as Trable finished with the bandage, Joel saw Volcan's ear twitch. Slowly the horse's visible eye opened and he began to stir.

"Volcan's alive!" Joel exclaimed as Trable helped him to his feet.

"Well, I'll be damned!" Trable said. "I reckon the bullet just creased him an' knocked him out."

They examined the big horse after the animal lunged to his feet. Trable was right. The bullet had just creased his neck behind the skull, stunning him. Volcan, sensing death in Dobel's still form on the ground, backed off snorting with the fear of death shared by all living things. Joel quieted him. They caught Dobel's horse that had stopped to graze nearby, and lashed his body to the saddle. Then they headed back to camp with their grim burden.

The riders were still out gathering cattle when they reached camp, where they found Pop Keller and Shuffle preparing the stew for the evening meal.

"What in the livin' hell has happened now?" Pop demanded in his croaking voice.

Joel told his rehearsed story about finding Dobel dead from a kick in the head.

"An' I suppose the same hoss got his teeth into your shoulder?" Pop asked suspiciously.

Joel thought quickly. "Naw," he improvised, "we was ridin' hell for leather after a fractious dogie through some juniper trees. A branch snagged my shoulder. It ain't nothin' to worry about."

"Dobel rode outta camp with Giles this mornin'. Where's Giles?"

"I don't know where, Pop, we never seen him."

Pop still wasn't satisfied. There was some more

sparring with words and then Joel decided tell the truth. He told the story in detail.

"Will you stick with the story I told you, Pop? You been with the BB a long time. I reckon I can trust you to play dumb until things work out."

"I ain't much for falsifyin', son, but I'll tell it your way. Your pa was never one to lurk behind a lie. He'd come right out an' let the fat hit the fire an blister whoever was guilty. But you're boss, now that Sam is locked up. Put the corpse in the shade of the supply wagon an' cover it with a tarp. We'll bury it in the cool of the night."

The men came into camp at sundown with their bunches of cattle. At first nobody spotted the covered corpse by the supply wagon. Giles came in late, alone and with no cattle. He was agitated and in a bad humor.

"That damfool Dobel," he sputtered, "cut himself out some cattle and run off with them. We're not far from the reservation. I suppose he hoped to sell them to the agent."

Dana came over and his toothy smile was nowhere in evidence. "What was that you said, boss?"

"I said Bull was a low-down thief. He ran off with some of the cattle and never showed up again," Giles said belligerently.

"You happen to be talkin' about one of my friends, boss. Ain't you the one who suggested siphonin' off a few cows to be stashed away for a later profit?"

A dead silence followed Dana's accusation. Joel watched Giles's reaction and Giles turned his eyes away.

Finally Giles replied, "I'm not stealing cattle, Dana.

I'm just equalizing a situation that Bruce Badly rigged to his advantage. Sam was trying to be tougher than his father. I was under the thumb of one Badly for years. Now Bruce is in jail. I don't intend to knuckle down to Sam. I'm going to run my own affairs from here on, and I'm just trying to make a fair start. I think Joel can understand that."

Joel pushed the hat back on his head and stood with his long legs braced. "I can't understand crookedness, Uncle Earl. We've been havin' a fair count here in camp, an' I see no cause for you to pad your tally. If Dobel ran off some of the cattle, he did it with your knowledge an' consent."

"Don't get snotty with me, Joel. Your standing here don't count for much. You're still a felon, a man disenfranchised by law," Giles charged.

"We'll let Dobel speak for hisself," Dana broke in. "He'll be back. He wouldn't traipse off by hisself."

Joel looked Dana in the eye. "He's already back, Pete, but I'm afraid he can't speak for himself."

"What kind of talk is that?" Giles interposed, sleeving the sweat off his high forehead.

"Plain talk, Uncle Earl," Joel replied, and he turned to Dana. "Do you want to know where Bull is, Pete?"

"Stop fudgin', Badly. Where is Dobel?"

"He's over by the supply wagon under that tarpaulin," Joel proclaimed.

There was a moment of tense silence. Then Dana asked, "Drunk?"

"See for yourself, Dana," Joel advised.

As Dana, fists clenched, walked toward the canvas-covered lump by the supply wagon, the eyes of the men followed him. He hesitated before throwing back the tarpaulin, as though sensing the truth. Then he jerked the tarp off and stared down at Dobel's lifeless form with its head bashed in. He let out a mighty oath and stalked toward the men. He faced Joel.

"Some lowlife ambushed him an' beat his brains out!" Dana shouted.

"Hold it, Pete!" Joel yelled back, watching Dana's gun hand. "Dobel was tromped by a horse. Take a good look at his head, an' you'll see the marks of a horse's shoe."

They examined the head of the dead man, and the mark of the calks of a horseshoe and the curve of the iron were visible after his head had been partly shaved.

Pop Keller, presiding over the steaming kettles on the stove, called to them, "Do you aim to bury the Bull before you eat, or after?"

Shuffle, his eyes gleaming white, shuffled over. "If'n you don't mind, ah'll dig a pit an' bury Mistah Dobel with the help of one volunteeh. Ah've been raised with a propah respect foh the dead."

Dutch Leiberg spoke up. "I'll give Shuffle a hand. You men wash up an' eat your chuck. Don't the burial party rate a shot of red-eye to ease their mind?"

Pop Keller reluctantly produced a bottle half full of whiskey. "There's a swaller for most of you, but don't look for no more."

The incident increased the tension between the two crews. Joel didn't mention the fact that *Sam* had been skimming cattle. He let that ride for Sam to bring up when the time was right.

By the time they reached Carrizozo near the towering Sierra Blanco Peak, which marked the northern end of the Mescalero Indian Reservation, the men's tempers were honed to a fine edge. As it was the last leg of the roundup, the men were given time off for a night on the town. Determined to have no more trouble, Joel again insisted the men leave their guns in camp. As a precaution he visited the sheriff when they reached town and reported that his men were unarmed. He couldn't vouch for Giles's crew as, since Dobel's death, they had become clannish and celebrated in a saloon of their choosing apart from the BB crew.

At the sheriff's office, Joel was stunned by momentous news. His father had escaped some days ago from the federal prison at Yuma and had killed a guard in the process.

"I'll be damned!" Joel exclaimed. "I can't blame Pa for escapin', but the killin' of the guard shows how desperate he was. That prison is a burnin' hell with caves dug into the hills an' iron bars to remind a man he's a caged animal. Have they got any trace of him?"

"No. I was telegraphed to be on the lookout for him." The sheriff added, "Mebbe he went to Mexico. That's close by Yuma."

Joel pondered this, but he rejected it. Pa would try to get home and clear himself of the charge of murdering Jim Costly. But the killing of the prison guard was an insurmountable obstacle. It was an act of desperation. Could the relentless heat of the sun have addled his father's brains?

He left the sheriff's office half dazed by the news. He thought of Sam in Carlsbad and went to the telegraph office in the stage depot and sent a wire to Sam. Sam had to know about their father's escape. The wire was a long one, and Joel went to a bar for a beer while he waited for an answer. When the answer came it muddled the situation further. According to the wire, Sam had been let off at a preliminary hearing and was heading for the roundup with his mother, who had come to Carlsbad to plead his case. Joel relayed the information to Archy Trable.

"When Sam gets here, Arch, there may be trouble. If the skimmin' of the cattle comes out in the open, there could be hell to pay. Things are pretty touchy right now. My Uncle Giles is a bitter man. He resented my pa, an' he was resentful of Sam. If he knew Sam was on his way here, it's hard to say what he might do."

"You better keep it under your hat, amigo. If Giles knowed Sam was comin' he might try something impossible to handle. Dana's got a bad taste in his mouth from that fight in Vado, an' Bull Dobel's death ain't sweetened it none. He'd be glad for an excuse to gun you down protectin' his boss's interest."

Joel agreed with Trable's assessment of the situation. He kept the fact of his father's escape from prison to himself. It would only increase the tension in camp if he told about it. After all, Bruce might never show up at the roundup. His only real chance of survival was to slip over the border at San Luis and remain in Mexico until the death of Jim Costly and the prison guard had become only dim memories.

Being near the Mescalero Reservation, Joel decided to call on the agent, Hyrum Eaton. There had been a tentative arrangement made with Eaton that he keep track during the year of the cattle being taken by the Indians and pay for them when an accounting was requested.

At the office of the agent, Joel was in for another surprise. Orson Giles, who had changed his name to

Miles, was there with his Indian wife, White Feather. Joel was glad to see him, and he marveled at the beauty of his Indian wife.

"I'm sure glad to see you, Orson. How come you happen to be here?"

"I'm making a routine audit of accounts here, and White Feather is checking on the girl from the convent who is in charge of the Indian school on the reservation."

"White Feather," Joel said, "I'm happy to meet you. You're beautiful."

"But I'm an Indian," she said quietly. "Only white girls are beautiful."

Joel shook his head. "Beauty isn't the color of one's skin, the slant of their eyes, or the texture of their hair. Beauty goes deeper than that. Orson was smart enough to know that." All at once his thoughts turned to another girl. "I—I have a cousin who is studyin' at the convent in Sante Fe. Her name is Margo."

"I told her about you and Margo, Joel," Orson confessed.

"You loved her very much, didn't you?" White Feather said.

Joel didn't answer. He had a lump in his throat and he didn't trust himself to speak.

White Feather, as though understanding his emotion, spared him the effort. "Why is it love must bring unhappiness?" she said softly. "I explained this to Orson before we married, but he insisted on going through with the ceremony."

"It brought me no unhappiness, darling," Orson said. "It brought me wisdom and patience to forgive men who call me squaw-man."

Joel explained he was at the reservation to check up on the stolen cattle. He went on to tell of everything that had happened on the roundup: of Sam's incarceration at Carlsbad, and of his being cleared of the charge of murder.

"Sam's on his way with our mother, who was at the hearing in Carlsbad and pleaded in Sam's behalf. Here's a shocker. My pa broke jail at Yuma an' killed a guard."

"Where did *you* hear that?" Orson asked.

"From the sheriff in Carrizozo," Joel replied.

"I know about that, Joel. I was hoping to keep it from you for the time being. You've got your hands full. I'm a deputy marshal. It gives me authority on my job. I've got orders to arrest your pa if I catch him. I was hoping to find him and get him to surrender."

"Bruce Badly surrender? Not until hell freezes over. And Uncle Giles is awful stubborn, too, Orson. He fretted under Pa's heavy hand. When Pa was in jail, he figgered to take over his place. But now he has Sam to deal with, an' Sam is out to prove he's just as tough as Pa was, or tougher." He didn't mention the skimming of the cattle. That could be remedied.

"Yes, my pa is tough under his mild exterior," Orson said. "He proved it when he disowned me. He didn't know he was doing me a favor. He was convinced I'd rot away without either Indians or white men for friends. Instead, I got an education and an important job, and my wife is respected by both the Indians and the white people."

"I've got to get back to camp, Orson. Maybe you can help me with the tally by the agent here. We'll be lucky to be paid for half the take."

CHAPTER THIRTEEN

The cavvy put in four hard days near Carrizozo, rounding up the cattle, branding the slicks, and doctoring the bull calves. Before breaking up the camp, Joel paid another visit to the agent of the reservation. Orson was still there, and he had worked out an equitable settlement for the cattle appropriated by the Indians. He gave Joel a government voucher for a sizeable amount.

"This will cover some of the losses," Orson said. "There's no way to pin down the exact number of beef lost to the Indians, and Hyrum Eaton will no doubt pad this bill when he sends it in, but the Indians figure they're entitled to some cattle for the loss of their land and the wild game that roamed it. As far as Hyrum goes, without a few fringe benefits it would be impossible to get an agent to take his job."

"That's all right with me, Orson. When are you goin' to make peace with your pa an' take your rightful name?"

"That's up to Pa. He's the one who kicked *me* out," Orson said pointedly.

"We'll be makin' our last gather near Tularosa on the road from Santa Fe to El Paso. You could stop off there an' make a stab at patching things up with Earl," Joel suggested.

"I'd have to get White Feather to agree to that. Indians are proud," Orson reminded him.

"So is your pa. With Margo gone, probably never to return, the Box-G is goin' to be a lonely place, Orson. Think it over."

They set up camp between the foothills of the Sacramento Mountains and alkali flats. The chill of coming winter permeated the high, thin air but there was no snow. The roundup here proved to be a slow, wearing thing. Some of the water holes had dried up during the summer and the cattle were wandering about between the salt licks and the few live springs that remained. When the two camps were set up independently, as usual, Giles came over to talk to Joel. He had Pete Dana with him. Joel braced himself for trouble.

"Uncle Earl," Joel said flatly, "you don't need no bodyguard to come here an' talk with me."

"Dana's not my bodyguard," Giles retorted. "I'm sure I can take care of myself."

Giles had lately been wearing a gun tied low on his thigh like a gunfighter.

Joel pointed to it. "Are you sure, uncle, that your sportin' a shootin' iron won't get you in trouble? I ain't never seen you fan a gun."

For answer Giles made a surprisingly fast draw and sent a bullet into the center of a juniper stump some twenty yards away. The shot aroused the men in camp and started what cattle were gathered to milling about. He looked at Joel with a smug defiance.

"That was a damfool thing to do!" Joel admonished him.

"Well, just remember you saw it, nephew. I always tried to be a man of law. But there's two kinds of law. I've practiced both of them. Before the courts came here, I was able to take care of myself. Ask your pa about it if you ever go to visit him in Yuma."

"Get to the point, Uncle Earl. What's in your craw now?"

"I'll tell you what's in my craw. First I had Bruce to push me around. Then Sam came along trying to be tougher than your father. Now they're both in jail and I'm still free. I ain't going to let you, a legal felon, take up where they left off. It's come to my attention that Sam has been cutting out some of the cattle and hiding them along the way."

"Who brought that to your attention, Uncle Earl? Was it Pete Dana here?" Joel indicated Dana, who was standing placidly by.

"Sure it was me, Badly. Fact is, I can lead you back to some of them cattle," Dana said evenly.

"You mean like the ones Bull Dobel was rustlin'?" Joel goaded him.

"You killed the wrong man, Badly. Dobel was under orders," Dana said.

"I didn't kill anybody!" Joel denied. "Whose orders was Dobel carryin' out, yours?"

"Do you want to tell him, Mr. Giles, or shall I?" Dana asked Earl.

"Did you come over to pick a fight, Uncle Earl?" Joel inquired.

"When I learned Sam was cutting out some of the cattle to be picked up later for the benefit of the BB, I decided to play at the same game, to square things." Giles glared at Joel belligerently.

"You gave the order for Dobel to cut out those cows, Uncle Earl?"

"I told you you killed the wrong man," Dana reminded him.

"I told you I didn't kill anybody. I saw you an' Dobel drivin' some cattle up a deep draw, but at first I couldn't recognize you, Uncle Earl. I rode closer for a better look an' was shot when I rode to the top of a sand hill. Before I could gather my senses, my horse lunged, terrified by it all. I was thrown from the saddle an' kicked in the head by one of Volcan's thrashing feet. Trable saw Dobel tryin' to steal Volcan, but Volcan knocked him down and tromped him. But not before Dobel got off a shot that struck Volcan behind the head, stunning him."

"That's your story, Badly," Dana retorted. "I ain't been known for my patience, Mr. Badly. I'm a Texas-border breed an' a man with too much patience didn't live long there. I've stretched a point with you—two points. What happened to Dobel ain't soothed me none. As you said yourself, the fight in the Vado Queen was a draw. One of these days we'll have to rectify that. Let's hope that day don't come too soon. I ain't been so kindly to a mollycoddled jailbird before."

Giles broke up the palaver. "Dana, I'm payin' you extra to take orders and a dollar a head bonus for the cattle you bring in that belong to me. Keep your grudge under your skin until the roundup's over. Then you can raise all the hell you want to short of outright murder. We ain't on the Texas border here, so you could end up in Yuma Prison with Bruce Badly."

Joel looked at his uncle. Earl Giles was turning into a bitter, vindictive man. He had more reason for it than Bruce's domination; he had the feeling of guilt for turning out his only son because of prejudice and false pride. He had the knowledge that his wife had taken Margo away from him to be made into a proud lady he might never see again. Such things galled and soured a man, but his uncle had brought it upon himself.

"Let's call a truce, Uncle Earl, until the roundup's over. I figger I can keep my men in line," Joel suggested.

"I can keep my men in line one way," Giles replied. "We'll keep the cattle we gather in separate herds. I'll do my branding over yonder toward the salt flats, an' you can brand the cattle you gather nearer the foothills. That way we'll keep the men apart. Their dispositions are rubbing pretty thin. We can combine our tallies when the job's done and make the split."

Joel agreed to the plan, but he didn't relish it. The roundup had never gone so badly before when Bruce had been in the ramrod's spot. Joel blamed himself for what was happening now, but he could see no other way to handle things without an open break. During the next two days as the two herds of cattle grew, a sudden change had come in the weather. A warm, moist chinook wind had blown up from the southwest and by some quirk of instinct it made the cattle uneasy. The men on the night watch crooned their cowboy songs to quiet them. Clouds, dark and threatening, came with the wind. In the dark of the night, without warning, a dry thunderstorm broke loose. The rumble of the thunder shook the ground, and the lightning flashes lit up the earth with an eerie light. Joel crawled out of his blankets. He heard some of the men cursing at being awakened from their sleep by the commotion. Trable, sleeping near Joel, got up.

"What the hell's goin' on, amigo?" he asked, standing close to Joel.

"Damned if I know," Joel replied. "We could be in for trouble!"

Other men stirred. Joel pulled on his boots, advising Trable to do the same. "There's goin' to be trouble, men!" he shouted. "Pull your boots on an' go for your horses! These dry lightning storms play hell with the cattle!"

The men, sleeping near the chuck wagon, were down near the creek. The cattle they had gathered were west of them away from the creek. Beyond their herd was Giles's herd, separated by a few hundred yards, not over a quarter of a mile. As the men headed for the remuda, an earth-shaking roll of thunder and a swordlike slash of lightning opened the gates of hell! There was a distant sound of cattle bawling and hooves pounding the dry ground.

Joel realized that Giles's herd had been spooked and was stampeding toward them. Their only hope was to hold their own herd in check and hope to break the onrush of Giles's herd. He didn't take time to strap on

his gunbelt. Every minute counted. He snatched his
gun from the holster and shoved it into his pants. The
men were rushing for the remuda. Joel hesitated, then
turned to look at the chuck wagon. Pop was inside
sleeping. The night lantern hanging at the side of the
wagon to keep away prowling animals burned like a
jewel in the ominous dark. He shouted at the wagon.
The growing noise of the onrushing cattle swallowed
up his words. He had no time to tarry. He turned and
took out after the other riders, praying for Pop's safety.

His delay had been fatal. The herds had combined
into one big knot of terrified flesh and bone. He could
never cross the front of it! He turned and ran blindly
ahead of the herd, hoping to reach the cottonwoods on
the other side of the creek. He ran a hundred yards with
the pound of hooves and the grunts of terror gaining on
him. His high-heeled boots were not made for racing
over uneven ground. He began to breathe in ragged
sobs, searching in the dark for any shelter—a rock, a
tree, a hole in the ground.

The heel of Joel's boot caught on a rock and twisted
his ankle. Pain shot up his leg. He fell to his knees.
Then he tried to get up. To lay there meant to be
trampled by the sharp, battering hooves. He half rose,
stumbled forward, and fell over the cutbank, four feet
high, that marked the flood stage of the creek. He
huddled back against the cutbank. The horde of frantic
cattle poured over the cutbank. Some of them fell to
their knees as they made the unexpected four-foot
drop. The others surged on over the bodies of the fallen
cattle. A steer slid over the bank, pinning Joel against
the wall of the bank. Scrambling to rise, the steer flailed
out with all four feet. One of the hooves struck him in

the side of the head. Unconsciousness delivered him from the hell of terror that flowed over him.

When he came to, the sound and fury had passed and he could hear men shouting excitedly. He dragged himself up over the bank and looked around. The chuck wagon was burning! He rose to his feet unmindful of his sprained ankle. Pop Keller slept in the chuck wagon and his hearing was not too good. When he reached the scene of the fire, Shuffle was dazedly scooping what water was left in the overturned water barrel and throwing it at the dying flames. Other men were beating at the flames with whatever they found handy.

"My God! My God!" Joel groaned. He could see Pop nowhere. "Where's Pop?"

"Ah reckon he's in that burnin' hell!" Shuffle shouted. "Ah slept under the supply wagon. It turned over an' I scrounged behind it for protection. That's all ah could do. The lantern set the chuck wagon on fire!"

When the flames burned low enough, Joel hobbled over the embers, his fists clenched. Pop lay in his blanket, a charred body covered with the brown residue of burned flour. Joel let out a sob and stood rigid. Tom Crawley shoved him aside with his long arm. He brushed the brown residue of flour away and exposed Pop's gray, balding head. The big flour barrel was against it. The head was cocked at an odd angle. Joel closed his eyes and waited for Crawley's verdict. Crawley and Pop had become close friends at the BB.

Crawley stood up. "I reckon they was some mercy in the situation," he said gravely, gulping back his emotion. "Pop didn't burn to death. The flour barrel hit him when the wagon turned over an' broke his neck."

A grim silence fell over the men standing at Pop's funeral pyre.

"Ah reckon ah'll clean him off, Mr. Badly," Shuffle said. "Yo'all go rest your bones. It's been a bad night. But fust he'p me right this supply wagon."

In the morning Shuffle managed to cook breakfast from the undamaged supplies in the wagon. Pop's body lay to one side, his face and head having been cleaned of the burned flour that had protected the skin. He looked like a mummy with the tarpaulin wrapped tightly about his body and his exposed face the color of worn leather. The lightning storm had subsided as suddenly as it had begun. The stampede had been stopped by the cottonwood trees across the creek, and the cattle were grazing quietly. Some cattle had been killed running into the trees, and a few were trampled to death near the cutbank which had saved Joel's life. Joel's ankle was not as sore as he had feared. He surveyed the situation and doggedly faced the men who were still groggy from the night's action. "The cattle are docile now. How about we bury Pop before the sun gets to him?"

Giles, arriving on the scene with his men, heard the suggestion. "We won't do no such thing. We'll gather the cattle first and bring them back where they belong. Pop can stand a few more hours above ground. He'll spend enough time in hell."

Giles's callous remark seethed into Joel's brain. "If Pop goes to hell, there ain't no chance for you, Uncle Earl!"

"Don't be so touchy, Joel. You're only a nincompoop jailbird," Giles jeered.

Confused by grief and weariness, Joel curbed his anger. This was no time for an open quarrel. They gathered the cattle and herded them back to the open ground near the branding fires. It was near noon when the job was done. When Joel rode back toward the stage road that ran near the camp, he was surprised to see Sam riding toward him at a fast trot. He hurried to meet him. Sam dismounted when Joel was close to him.

"What in the living blazes happened here?" Sam demanded.

"That lightning storm boogered the herds. Giles didn't stop his herd, an' it ran into our herd. They stampeded for the creek." Then Joel explained everything else that had happened.

"Pop Keller's dead? The chuck wagon burned?" Sam barked.

"We ain't had nothin' but bad luck and trouble since we left Carlsbad. I heard that Ma helped get you out of jail there. Where is she now?"

"She stopped in Carrizozo to wait for the stage from Santa Fe to Vado. What's all this trouble you mentioned?"

"It's Uncle Earl. He figgers that with Pa locked up, he's the boss of the Tularosa Range. He sets up his camp away from ours. He's got his own brandin' fire, an' when the job's done, we compare tallies an' split the take. I ain't sure his tally is fair. He's cursed Pa, he's cursed you, an' he figgers I don't count for nothin' because I'm a felon."

Sam's face became a grim mask. "Pa ain't locked up no more, Joel. He kilt a guard an' escaped from Yuma. I heard about it in Carrizozo. He's headed for hell for sure now."

"I also heard about it in Carrizozo, Sam. I reckon

Pa's takin' a detour to hell. I figger he crossed the border into Mexico near Yuma. He was next door to hell in that prison. I *know*," Joel said grimly.

"Ma might have somebody else with her on the stage," Sam said. "We ran into Orson Giles in Carrizozo. His pa kicked him out years ago for marryin' a Indian girl. He's changed his name—"

"I know all about that, Sam. Orson kept Pete Dana from killin' me durin' the fight in the Vado Queen. He asked me to keep his identity a secret. I met his wife in Carrizozo. There ain't many women can equal her for looks and intelligence."

"I agree. Ma is trying to talk them into coming back to the ranch with her. She's convinced he should make up with Earl, and that Earl would accept White Feather once he knew her."

"I don't know about a reconciliation. Earl is actin' crazy. He figgers to get even with Pa for bossin' him all these years. Now he's turned his hate on you. He aims to split off from the Badlys completely an' run his own affairs. I reckon the fact that he banished his only son has come back to haunt him.

"And now that Elsa has taken Margo to Santa Fe, perhaps never to come back, Earl is a lonely, desperate man. What's a man got to live for if he ain't got no kin to leave his worldly goods to? I wouldn't blame Orson if he never came back. Margo won't be back, that's for sure. She'll marry some dude and be an uppity lady. Another girl has gone to Santa Fe. I hope she meets Margo. They could help each other."

"What other girl do you mean, Joel?"

"Dorothy Layton, the school ma'am's niece. She came West to get over a broken heart an' wounded pride." He went on to tell of his long conversation with Dorothy and her daring journey by boat and stage to get to Santa Fe. Then he came back to the present situation. "Earl's takin' to wearin' a gun, Sam. He gave me a demonstration of his ability to use it."

"Wearin' a gun could get him killed, Joel. He might fancy hisself a dead-shot, but he ain't never faced a fast gun. That was left up to Pa. Pa used his gun once too often. That's why Jim Costly is dead."

"But Pa didn't mean to kill him!" Joel said defensively.

"I'm not sure about that, either," Sam said in a flat, humorless voice.

There was a cloud of dust approaching as Giles and two of his men rode toward them. Even from the distance they could see the twisted fury on Earl Giles's face as he recognized Sam.

"Hell's about to break loose," Joel warned, feeling for his own gun as he saw Dana riding beside Giles, with Leiberg just behind them.

CHAPTER FOURTEEN

Joel dismounted and stood beside Sam as Giles, Dana, and Dutch Leiberg approached. Joel looked down at his gun but kept his hand away from it. "It don't look good, Sam. Dana's promised to finish the fight we had in the Vado Queen, an' he blames me for Dobel's death. Uncle Giles ain't goin' to be happy to see you back here either."

"We'd better split up, Joel," Sam cautioned. "Move over close to that bank of chaparral that leads up from the road. Where's the BB crew?"

"They're over yonder, workin' the herd. They can't see us for the dust. Anyway, we don't want no massacre," Joel said as he walked toward the thick clump of chaparral. He kept his eyes on Dana and

179

Leiberg. He could see by the set of their shoulders and
the hang of their guns that they meant business.

"I'll handle Earl," Sam said as Joel walked away.
"He'll cower down when he sees I mean to take over. I
reckon he was always a mite scared of Bruce. Now he
sees Bruce in me."

Joel stopped about forty feet from Sam, his back
against the thick tangle of mesquite, cacti, and
sagebrush. He could hear clearly what was being said.

Dana called to Joel, "You gittin' ready to scamper
into the chaparral like a brush rabbit, Badly?"

Leiberg spoke up, his skinny body loose in the
saddle. "You want I should head him off, Pete?"

Giles spoke in a harsh, grating voice. He sounded
like a stranger, as though some evil spirit had entered
his body. "Shut up, you two!" he said to Dana and
Leiberg. "I'm still boss here and I mean to remain
boss!"

"You're kiddin' yourself, Mr. Giles," Dana retorted
in a jeering voice. "You couldn't boss a litter of new-
borned pups. We all been salvin' you up, hopin' to line
our own pockets. Even Joel Badly, the fuzzy-chin kid
has been coddlin' you. Look ahead, theah's Bruce
Badly's son, Sam. Try givin' him orders. If you want to
make yourself king of the Tularosa, you better be
prepared to back them orders up. It'll take more than
blabber to cower him."

Giles trembled with pent-up emotion under Dana's
harsh indictment, but he didn't reply to it. He swung
out of the saddle, facing Sam on even ground. Dana
and Leiberg also dismounted, spreading out. Joel
remained where he was with the chaparral at his back.
He watched the deadly drama building up before his

eyes but was powerless to stop it. The stampede had been the catalyst to bringing to a head all of the smoldering hate, greed, and resentment that had dogged the roundup like a pack of jackals waiting for the kill.

Dana was choosing this moment to finish the fight in the Vado Queen, to assuage his wounded pride and destroy Joel, who had battered him senseless before the cheering men who had waited long to see him humbled. This time there would be no one to interfere with the execution.

Giles's voice broke into Joel's thoughts. "Why in the living blazes did you have to come back, Sam Badly? They should've hung you in Carlsbad, just like they should've hung your father and your brother. I've got your father's boot off my neck! You're not going to put your foot there in his place!"

Then the weird miracle happened. Threshing his way out of the chaparral at Joel's back, guns strapped to his thighs and the hat gone from his shaggy, iron gray head, charged an apparition with a half-grown beard and the blaze of hell in his piercing eyes. Joel felt a huge hand squeeze his emotions into a knot. The apparition was Bruce Badly, his father!

"You're damned right, Earl! Sam won't need his foot on your neck 'cause mine ain't never been off! It was you got me jailed! Not because you love justice as you pretend, but because you hate me and wanted revenge! Maybe I wanted to kill Jim Costly, maybe I didn't. Maybe the devil guided my hand. I was tired of Jim comin' over to my place teachin' Joel how to shoot an' ride, things *I* should've been teachin' him, and then treatin' Kay as though she was something special to him. I reckon you egged Jim on because you knew the truth an' wanted to crucify me with it. I'm back, Earl. What are you goin' to do about it?"

"You ain't goin' to stay back, Bruce! You're a murderer, a bully, and condemned by your own folly!" Giles screamed.

Giles clawed desperately for his gun. Bruce's hand lashed down for one of the guns he had picked up at the ranch on his way out here.

"No—no!" Joel barked. "It can't end this way!"

He threw himself in front of his father just as Giles's gun roared. Joel knocked his father's gun aside and felt the shock of Giles's bullet in his own side. Bruce shoved Joel away. Sam lunged at Giles, hoping to knock him down, but Bruce's gun barked once—twice! Sam let out a grunt as the bullets hit him. He clawed at Giles, taking him down with him as he fell. Joel managed to stagger to his feet. He saw Dana grinning maliciously, his buck teeth showing white.

"All right, Joel, let's clear the record while we're at it. Go for your gun!" Dana yelled. Leiberg stood braced beside him.

Joel centered his gaze on Dana. He had to kill Dana. He couldn't kill them both, and Leiberg had his hand on his gun ready for the draw. The thought of Dana forcing his attentions on Margo guided his hand in a snakelike draw and held the gun steady as he fired at Dana once, twice, three times! Dana fell to his knees and pitched forward on his face, firing as he fell. Joel felt the weight of Dana's bullets in him but no pain—he was past feeling pain. Through bleary eyes he looked for Leiberg. The roar of Leiberg's gun still echoed in his mind. Leiberg was flat on his back, arms outflung. Joel felt himself weakening. He looked for his father. Bruce

Badly lay on his side, his gun still pointed at Leiberg.

Vaguely Joel realized his father had saved him from Leiberg's gun and had taken the bullets meant for him. He dropped to his knees, looking for Sam and Giles. They lay one on top of the other in the familiar, ugly pose of death. He couldn't believe his eyes! The completeness of the slaughter wrenched a sob from his throat. He was the only one alive!

"My God—my God—my God!" he groaned, a sob choking him. "Take me, too," he whispered. "Take me, too." Then he fell like the others. He didn't hear the shouts and the footbeats of the men running over from the herd.

When Joel came to, he found himself lying in the shade of a stagecoach. His mother's face was hovering over him. It was all unreal. He was floating on a cloud of pain. He closed his eyes quickly. This was all part of the horrible nightmare he had dreamed. He opened his eyes again. His mother's face was still there. He was aware of the blankets swaddling him. He didn't want to go back into that horrible nightmare again.

His own voice sounded strange. "Where—where am I? Is—is that you, Ma? Am I home? I hurt, Ma. I had a horrible dream of killing and killing and killing!"

"Lie quietly, son," Kay Badly crooned, laving his hot forehead with water.

He was aware of people milling about. There was a paunchy man in a white shirt and silk tophat standing near the stagecoach. He was rummaging in a black bag. He took out a bottle and put it to Joel's lips.

"Who are you?" Joel asked suspiciously, pushing the bottle away.

"I'm Dr. Elroyd. You were lucky that I was on the

stagecoach. Now take a sip of this brandy, it will help you. I had to dig for those bullets."

"Give it to me, Doctor," Kay said. "He's still in shock. Let me give it to him."

He gulped the fiery liquor and it jarred him into full consciousness. The terrible truth of what had happened caused him to cry out, "My God—my God— they're all dead! Ma! Ma! Do you hear me?"

"I hear you, Joel. *You're* not dead," Kay said in a shaky voice.

"Why ain't I dead? Sam an' Pa, they're dead. Giles is still alive, ain't he? He started the massacre, an' no bullet touched him," Joel said savagely.

"No, no bullet touched him, Joel, but the hand of justice did. Tom Crawley told me what happened. Sam took the bullets your father meant for Giles. Bruce saved your life by killing Leiberg, but was killed in the process. You killed Dana. Don't fret over Bruce. He was a condemned man. He killed a guard at Yuma."

"An' what about Uncle Earl?" Joel asked.

"He died of a heart attack caused by the excitement," Kay said grimly.

"They're better off than me, all of them. I'll have to live and be haunted by this terrible day for the rest of my life. Nobody can help *me*!"

"I can help you, Joel," a soft voice said.

He saw a beautiful face framed in shining blonde hair. It was another vision. He was being plagued with visions. The next minute the vision was down beside him, and Margo's lips were hungrily seeking his.

"I love you—I love you—I love you, Joel," she repeated joyfully. The others drew back giving them a moment of privacy.

"I—I love you too, Margo, but why torture ourselves? Nothing can come of it," he said in a husky voice.

"Oh, but it can, darling. The Governor's wife, Leffa Demargo, was a close friend of your mother and my mother. She told me many things. Your ma married Uncle Bruce because he was strong and ambitious. When Sam was only five years old, Uncle Bruce was away most of the time, and Jim Costly was working for the BB then. He stayed at the ranch to run things when Pa and Uncle Bruce were away buying up land grants from the ignorant heirs for pennies on the dollar. They were building their herd with wild cattle, mavericks, and beef that sold for two dollars a head after the war. Aunt Kay was lonesome and she had come to resent Uncle Bruce's domineering ways. She fell in love with Jim Costly and had an affair with him from pure loneliness and neglect. You're not my cousin, Joel. Jim Costly was your father!"

The shock of her revelation numbed his mind. No wonder he had been fond of Jim Costly, and Jim Costly had been more than friendly with his mother. Kay Badly moved in close.

"I heard some of what Margo told you, son. Jim Costly *was* your father, but I didn't let on to Bruce or you or anybody but Leffa. I didn't want to hurt Bruce's pride, and I was afraid of his reaction if the truth came out. He was a man with a giant pride, trampling people underfoot to get his way. He finally became the victim of his own sins."

The confusion in Joel's mind overcame the pain of his bandaged wounds. It was no wonder that he had never felt close to Bruce.

"This all like a dream," Joel mused. "How come the stagecoach reached here just now?"

"It was on its regular schedule," Margo told him. "I was surprised when your mother boarded the stage at Carrizozo. We heard the sound of shots before we reached here. We were spared the sight of the killings, but we got here in time for the doctor to get the bullets out of your carcass and bandage you up. Aunt Kay brought somebody with her." Margo beckoned to someone who was talking to the stage driver.

Joel was mystified to find Orson and his wife, White Feather, looking down at him.

"How come you're here, Orson?" Joel asked.

"Aunt Kay insisted that I go back to Vado with her and try to patch things up with my father. Fate took that chore out of my hands. Looks like you and I are the only ones left to take over. I don't intend to give up my job, and White Feather still has the schools to look after. We'll consolidate the ranches again, one brand, and you can be the ramrod. We'll stop the roundup right here. The cattle will all belong to one herd anyhow. We'll haul Sam, Pa, and Uncle Bruce back to the ranch and bury them proper. Dana and Leiberg can be buried here."

"Pop Keller's body is wrapped up yonder by the supply wagon. We got to take him along," Joel declared. Then he looked at Margo, still unable to believe his love could be fulfilled. "Did you meet Dorothy Layton in Santa Fe?" he asked her.

"The day she arrived. She said she almost fell in love with you herself, but she had some things to straighten out. She decided to stay in Santa Fe and help the nuns at the convent. She put Porferio, the Mexican boy, in school there. My ma will be surprised to see me back at the ranch, but that's where I belong."

Joel reached out with his good arm and drew her close to him. "This is where you belong, sweetheart, right here in my arms." Then he met her warm sweet lips with his own. But soon a disturbing thought intruded into his magic moment.

"I ain't sure a felon can buy a marriage license, honey," he said ruefully.

"You're not a felon, honey. Judge Cottle felt uneasy about the sentence he was forced to give you. He requested the pardon of the Governor but wanted to keep it quiet because a judge nullifying his own verdict might cause talk. It was a full pardon. Leffa explained it to me. The warden at Yuma failed to explain that to you. You have the same rights as any other citizen."

Joel felt a glow of relief. This terrible showdown that had brought death to five men had one macabre virtue. It had destroyed all the jealousy, suspicion, and dissension that had cursed the Tularosa Range for so long.

Joel managed a smile. "I got one right no other man can ever have," he declared.

"What right is that, honey?" Margo asked softly.

"The right to love you until death do us part."

He felt the warmth of her cheek against his, moistened by the tears of happiness that she made no effort to restrain.